IN SHADOW VALLEY

Shadow Valley is a small, isolated and inconsequential farming community. However, within one of the ramshackle old farmhouses, some distance from the rest, dwells a power that threatens death and destruction to anyone discovering its secrets. Now the stability of the community is put at risk when Lila Ellis arrives. Working on a project to flood Shadow Valley and create a reservoir, she will enter the old Stevenson place alone . . . and alone she must face its terrors.

Books by Michael R. Collings
in the Linford Mystery Library:

DEVIL'S PLAGUE
SERPENT'S TOOTH

MICHAEL R. COLLINGS

IN SHADOW VALLEY

Complete and Unabridged

LINFORD
Leicester

First published in Great Britain

First Linford Edition
published 2013

British Library CIP Data

Collings, Michael R.
  In Shadow Valley. - -
  (Linford mystery library)
  1. Suspense fiction.
  2. Large type books.
  I. Title II. Series
  813.6–dc23

  ISBN 978–1–4448–1472–9

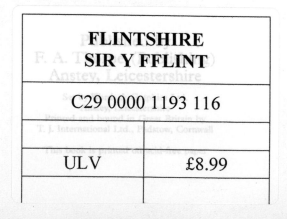

DEDICATION:

For Judi,
sine qua non

and for the original of
Aunt Annie,
who was NOTHING *like this one*

1

Lila Ellis was surprised to discover that she was afraid to approach the last door.

The fear surprised her as much as anything.

It wasn't as if she hadn't been doing this for the past two weeks. Yes, it was occasionally uncomfortable, but the last of the diehards had left nearly a month before, several escorted down-mountain by stone-faced Staties bearing official warrants as well as loaded side-arms. Even a rifle or two.

No, facing the anger, the resentment, the bottled-up fury wasn't the problem. By now the only hangers-on were the handful that hadn't yet signed the final papers. All of their possessions were gone by now, long since transported to greener — or at least *drier* — pastures . . . or, in several cases, deposited in swales and shallow valleys where they would remain until they gradually decomposed and became one with the sludge and slime that would form the bottom of the lake.

Shadow Valley Lake.

The final dams across the six or seven tributaries exiting Shadow Valley were nearly complete, awaiting only her signal that every legal *T* had been duly crossed, every *I* capped by its appropriate dot.

Tuttle's would be the last crosses and dots.

Well, the second-to-the last, to be truthful.

Lila shuddered at the thought of approaching the Stevenson place, even though she'd never even seen it. The stories she'd heard were enough to give the place a reputation for weirdness.

At least the shudder had one positive result.

Lila straightened up in her seat, stared fixedly out the front window for a few seconds, took a couple of deep breaths, and opened the car door.

Her movement seemed to break a stasis that had settled over the Turtle place the moment she had turned into the long, rutted drive. Poplars — some of the last trees remaining in the valley — that had seemed more like grave-yard sentinels than living things suddenly began to whisper in the faint breeze, their leaves flickering from green to silver and back again with the rapidity of old-time telegraphers stuttering out their messages in Morse code.

She wondered what they were saying to each other.

Soon. Soon. Soon. And all will be dark and deep and quiet. Quiet. Quiet.

Perhaps.

Overhead, a dozen or so black dots spiralled against the deep blue sky. They were too far away for Lila to gauge size. They might have been sparrows, or crows . . . or even vultures gathering for a final feed.

Insects began wheezing in the chest-high weeds bordering the drive and spilling onto what should have been — three months earlier *would* have been — a neatly trimmed yard, with a patch of emerald grass surrounded by cut-flower borders in full riot of summer colors.

Even the rhythmic sound of the cicadas

seemed fraught with meaning.

As she stood for a moment in the growing heat, Lila tried to understand what they were saying, but meaning evaded her.

Only the job was real.

She sighed, reached back into her rental, and retrieved her briefcase. Not too long ago, it had been stuffed with sheaves of papers to be signed. Now it felt light in her grasp, almost empty.

She straightened and turned toward the old farmhouse.

It looked no different than any of the others she had been to over the past few days. Built decades before of hand-hewn lumber, with rough wooden shingles already beginning to look abandoned and forlorn, as if the next strong wind might pick them up and send them spinning across the valley, over the surrounding hills, and on to some new world that lay beyond.

A full-length porch shaded the front door. In the shadows, Lila saw someone standing, waiting, as patiently as Time itself.

For this house, Lila thought as she made her way along the walk way of rough slate slabs, *Time has run out*.

'Mr. Tuttle,' she called, trying to infuse her voice with just the right touch of somberness without sounding too much like a professional mortician about to try a hard-sell on a grieving widow.

The figure moved slightly. This was Mr. Tuttle.

'I'm Lila Ellis,' she said as she stepped into the welcome coolness of the porch. 'You may remember me from the . . . '

'I do.' Nothing more. Not a nod of greeting. Not a hand outstretched in the almost mandatory greeting of rural neighbours.

But then, she wasn't a neighbour.

If anything, she was the enemy.

'I've come to . . . '

'I know.' He turned his back on her and entered the house.

With another deep breath — and an even more powerful sense of discomfort — she followed.

The interior was no surprise. She'd seen it — or its sisters, cousins,

5

second-cousins-once-removed — on farm after farm throughout the valley. A living room. Large, open . . . empty of everything except one broken chair huddled in the corner. A door that might lead to the kitchen, which would have a single window overlooking the outbuildings — or rather where outbuildings once stood — and its own entrance/exit. Another door that might lead to several bedrooms tucked away on the quieter side of the house. And a third that would lead to the attic, emptied of everything except dust and ghosts and the dried-up bodies of bluebottle flies trapped there eons before and shriveled by the summer heat.

Lila didn't bother looking for a table. She almost automatically braced her briefcase on one hip while she opened it and took out the remaining papers.

'These are the . . . '

'I know.' Apparently Goodman Tuttle wasn't going to let her finish a sentence. He had taken control of the meeting before she had even set foot on the porch and he was not going to relinquish it.

It was his last controlling act over the

place that had been his family's for three generations.

She held the papers out to him. There were only two. A cover letter signed by the governor — or at least by the governor's automated signature machine; even Lila couldn't tell the difference any more and she doubted if the governor herself could — and a second sheet, its message shorter, more clipped, signed by the ranking local state police officer, adorned by a stamped gold seal, and lacking only Abraham Tuttle's signature to fulfill its purpose on earth.

Tuttle didn't even look at the papers. Time for that was long past. He simply took them, his face as stone-faced as the Staties' had been when they stared down his more rebellious neighbors, walked over to a wall, and, using it as a one-time desk, scribbled his signature.

Still without speaking, he turned and held them out to her.

'That all?'

Lila nodded.

He strode to the doorway and stepped through, formally relinquishing his farm, his history, his dreams, his life. He disappeared from the porch. From Lila's sight.

She stood there for a long time.

The house already smelled differently than it had a few moments before. Then, it had been owned, even if it was empty.

Now it was abandoned, slated to be leveled tomorrow by an onslaught of bulldozers and backhoes. The remains would be carried away and deposited in a landfill — actually, a nearby canyon that boasted neither arable soil nor slopes suitable for winter skiing or summer hiking. Or, if the surveyor gave his approval, what was left of the house might simply be left there for the water to bury, assuming that would be at a sufficient depth not to interfere with the projected influx of boaters and water-skiers that would turn the dead valley into a recreational paradise.

Supposedly.

Lila listened.

Nothing.

Not a creak or groan from an ancient joint. Not a rattle of time-worn panes in weathered frames. Not even the scurrying of mice in the sudden emptiness.

Probably they had all moved out by now also, Lila decided.

'Oh well,' she said, abruptly aware of how loud her voice sounded. Then, more quietly, 'Oh, well.'

She walked out of the house, being perversely careful to close the front door softly but firmly. That much she had learned from her grandmother, dead over a decade now, who — she had always said — learned it from her own grandmother, who had once lived somewhere on the far side of Shadow Valley. Beyond that, Lila realized, she knew remarkably little about her family. Neither her mother nor her grandmother had been very forthcoming on the subject.

She might even have relatives — or have *had* relatives — in the valley, she thought for the dozenth . . . or perhaps the hundredth time. She didn't know. If so, they had long since dropped out of touch with her branch of the family.

The city branch.

The branch that had split and wound

its way through time, until finally she had bloomed at the furthermost tip of one small limb, city-bred, university-educated, official spokesperson and — truth be told — lackey for a government that had decided in its great wisdom that nearly two centuries of farming families, with all of their traditions, were of less value than one more reservoir to carry water to . . . the city.

She turned, made certain once again that the door was closed, then headed toward her car.

2

Lunch was a sandwich in the shade of the single standing wall of the old stone church at the crest of the rise. As always when she stopped there, Lila wondered what vagaries of the state planning officials had decreed that that one wall should remain upright. She could think of no good reason for it but, again as always, she was grateful for the relative coolness and the break from the sun beating down on the rest of the valley.

She had made the sandwich herself — tuna with pickles and Miracle Whip. She had never been able to develop a taste for mayonnaise, not after so many years of her mother's cooking with nothing but the creamy, tangy salad dressing.

Oh, well.

It had remained cold in the small ice chest that she had gotten into the habit of taking with her every time she had to come out to Shadow Valley. Once there had been a store of sorts where the main road split just to the north of the small settlement, a kind of poor-man's general store that carried a little bit of everything, not much of anything.

It had been out of business for nearly twenty years, she had been told by one of the long-time residents, who still used the blackened quarter acre where it had stood before fire had destroyed it as a point of reference: Just stop a hundred yards before you get to Aames's Store and you'll find them blackberries right along the roadway.

There had never been a Mickey-D's in Shadow Valley.

Never would be now.

Unless you counted the possibility that the Marina, scheduled to be built about a half-mile up the hillside, might someday merit its own fast-food haven.

But right now, all that Lila could count on was her small ice chest and its reserves of bottled water, four more sandwiches, and a bag of cookies from the Albertson's a block or so from her one-bedroom apartment.

Just in case.

She finished the sandwich, folded the empty plastic bag in half — *waste not, want not,* as her grandmother would have said — and stowed it inside the ice chest.

She fiddled with the controls on the driver's side of the rental until the seat reclined in just the right position, and settled back for a short nap.

The car was warm. The sun through the side window was warm.

All was well.

For the moment.

She did not dream.

When she woke, she was startled to find that she had not slept for the usual few moments.

Instead, the sun was well on its way toward the crest of mountains to the west. It wasn't twilight yet, not by a long ways, but there was a hint of golden brilliance to the light that suggested late afternoon.

'Oh no.' Her plan had been to take care of the last pieces of business and be home long before sunset.

So much for planning.

She had one final stop to make. Ideally

it would take even less time than she had spent at the Tuttle place, which itself had set a personal-best time for in-and-out.

Abraham Tuttle had barely spoken to Lila.

At the final stop, there would be no one to speak to her at all.

Probably.

She sighed again at the thought of the last house, checked her hand-drawn map of Shadow Valley, started the car, and pulled out of the shadow of the single, barren wall.

Main Street of Shadow Valley was a narrow gravel road, barely wide enough for two small cars to pass, certainly not wide enough for a car and a tractor or combine at the same time. That accounted for the wide borrow pits that separated the dusty roadway from the straggling remains of crumbling picket fences that had at one time surrounded neat front yards.

Lila followed Main — actually *Only Street* — until it dead-ended a mile to the south at a T-intersection. Along the way, she passed the remnants of three farms:

denuded fields where no one had bothered to plant for the last summer; century-old poplars lopped at the base and left like ancient monoliths where they lay; skeletons of homes and outbuildings rotting where they had fallen . . . or in one case, the blackened ash of the fire that had wiped out every other trace of the farm.

At the T-intersection, Lila turned left — east — and abandoned the main road for what seemed like little more than a cattle trail with an advanced degree. Bushes of yellow wild roses overhung the roadway on both sides, broken only here and there by even narrower driveways leading to abandoned farms. The roses were well past their prime flowering period, so even the remaining blooms seemed faded and despondent.

The road continued straight east for a mile or so before it began to meander, following the course of one of the larger streams that would ultimately be backed up to flood the valley. The roses, in such close proximity to moisture year round, grew thicker, denser. Where before Lila could catch occasional glimpses of pasturelands overgrown with thistles and runners from the hedges, all she could see now were dark green leaves, smudged petals, and occasional canes that, studded with wicked thorns, would shoot out across the road. She actually began to worry about whether or not the insurance on her rental would be good for scratches to the paint.

Even though the road itself had forced her to slow, she found herself almost stopping every time it twisted away to one side or the other, disappearing for the moment into the bushes. At times, it looked as if the road might simply dead-end at a hypertrophied mass that would finally deny her permission to drive further.

But each time, the turn revealed another bend in the road, another half-shaded passageway through the thorns.

At one of the turns, Lila angled the car just enough so that for an instant the sun behind her caught in her side-view mirror. It was as if the sun had exploded in her eyes. A sudden great flare of white-beyond-white, then a pain behind her eyelids. She almost brought both hands to her face to help shade her pupils from the unexpected glare but at the last moment gripped the wheel more firmly and kept the car from driving straight into one of the largest mounds of roses yet.

And straight into the woman standing there, mouth open in a cry of surprise, one hand held to her mouth as if to capture the cry and preserve it, the other clenched tightly on the bale of a small metal bucket.

'No!' Lila jammed on her brakes, still gripping the steering wheel. Mercifully, the sun chose that moment to slip beyond the mirror and the glare winked out as instantaneously as it had flashed.

Her eyes ached but Lila kept enough presence of mind to force the car to a halt, only a foot or so from the spot where the woman was standing. She had not moved a muscle. Her cry had died still-born.

When the car grated to a halt on the thin layer of gravel, Lila could hear nothing but silence around them. The engine had unaccountably died. Even Lila's own breathing seemed to have stopped, her heart to have discontinued momentarily its *thrum*-ing rhythm.

She sat still for another moment, then threw the car door open and rushed out.

'Oh, I'm so sorry! Are you hurt? Are you all right?'

In answer the other woman — older than Lila, perhaps some years older even than Lila's mother — lowered her hand from her mouth and smiled.

'Why, yes, dear. I'm perfectly fine. Just startled.'

'The car didn't . . . '

'Oh, no, you missed me by inches.' Something playful glittered in the older woman's eyes. 'You'll just have to try harder next time.'

'No,' Lila breathed, 'I mean, it was . . . the sun blinded me just as . . . oh, that was a joke.'

'Yes. Ill-timed perhaps but well meant. I truly am just fine. And you were going so slowly anyway that there was never any real danger. We're used to such meeting on these twisty old country roads.'

'I'm truly sorry. I was just looking for . . . '

'Not another word, my dear. Not to worry.' The older woman leaned slightly to place her bucket on the ground, then straightened and extended her hand.

Lila reached out and shook it. The grip was warm and firm. Friendly. A welcome change after the often frigid greetings she was used to in the Valley.

'I'm Lila. Lila Ellis.'

Again, Lila caught a glitter in the other woman's eyes, less playful this time, more . . . well, Lila wasn't quite certain, and it lasted for such a short time that, later, she couldn't quite recall how it had looked.

'*Lila.*' The woman smiled even more broadly. 'Such a lovely name. For a lovely girl.'

There was a brief pause. Lila felt as if she were being examined, if not under a microscope then at least under a high-power hand lens, the kind Sherlock Holmes might have carried tucked away in a deep pocket of his cloak for safe keeping.

'You may call me Ella,' the other woman said at last. She nodded slightly — to Lila, it felt as if the woman was giving *her* permission to be Lila Ellis . . . a kind of royal endorsement, as of Queen, or perhaps Queen Mother, to commoner. Still, the woman — *Ella*, Lila reminded herself — smiled widely enough to nearly eclipse the sun that was now threatening to slide beneath the rose hedges behind the car.

Lila felt herself blushing but before she could respond, Ella added, 'And you must have been looking for the Stevenson place.'

'Uh . . . yes, yes I was. How did you . . . ?'

'How did I know? Simple elimination. You passed the last farm — it used to belong to the Wards before the . . . before — anyway, you passed it a good quarter of a mile ago. And there is nowhere else to go on this road except the Stevensons'. It's around the next curve and over the top of that hill.'

Lila looked in the direction Ella had indicated and started to say something

. . . to thank her, but Ella forestalled the effort. 'I'd be glad to show you, if you don't mind having a gabbing old fool sitting in that pretty new car of yours.'

'Oh, it's not mine, it's a . . . ' Lila laughed, feeling rather like a giddy young fool at the moment. 'Was that another joke?' she added, pointing to the rental agency's prominent decal on the front window.

'Well, yes. You caught me again. But seriously, I would be happy to show you. The driveway's a bit jungly and you might miss it. Then you would have to follow this bit of a creek' — she pronounced it *crick*, just as the others in the Valley had — 'you might have to follow it for another five miles or so before you could turn around.'

'I would appreciate that. The last little while it's been like nothing existed except me, the car, and these infernal roses, getting thicker and thicker with each turn.'

'I know how you feel,' Ella said as she walked around to the passenger door and opened it. She barely had room to get

21

inside without being pricked by thorns. 'I grew up over there' — she made a vague gesture back toward the area of Main Street with her free hand. 'Even for us natives, the hedges can be a bit overwhelming in high summer. Especially when there's no one around to prune the growth the way it should be.'

Lila nodded, opened her own door, and slid behind the wheel. Ella was already seated, belted, and ready to go.

'Home, James,' Ella said in a mock-aristocratic tone, then added: 'To infinity . . . and beyond!'

Lila laughed, perhaps more than the joke deserved. She was more relieved at the outcome of her near collision. But she laughed anyway.

'Second star on the right . . . ,' Lila began.

'And straight on to morning,' Ella finished, without any break in the rhythm.

Still laughing, Lila turned the ignition key.

The car did not start.

The engine grumbled once, then fell silent.

'Not here,' Lila said. 'I don't . . . '

'Just give it a moment. Maybe it has to catch its breath, like we did.'

Lila glanced quizzically at Ella. That wasn't precisely the kind of automotive advice she was used to receiving.

After a minute or two, Ella nodded. 'Now.'

The engine turned over on the first try, and purring like a giant tiger on some unknown pathway rank with growth, the car rolled forward.

Like a forgotten memory, canting slightly on the uneven gravel, the small bucket rested by the side of the road.

3

Apparently Ella really did know Shadow Valley well, although, as she explained as they made their way through the thicket, she hadn't lived at the place back by Main Street for years and years. Even so, as soon as Lila guided the car in one final long, looping circle paralleling the creek — *crick* — maneuvered it through a sharp right-hand turn onto an almost invisible lane, and urged it to the top of a small rise, the two women found themselves looking down into a hollow.

It seemed deeper than the rest of Shadow Valley for some reason, with barely enough arable land for a couple of reasonable-sized fields and a large frame house. The house was more weathered than the rest Lila had seen, and, although it had at least two stories, it seemed almost to crouch beneath the thick branches of two huge box-elders. Neither had yet been scarred by axe or saw, and the scattered outbuildings were similarly untouched.

'Perhaps it will be deep enough here that they won't have to pull the buildings down,' Lila said, more to herself than to her companion.

'Perhaps.'

'I'm not sure that I would want to live out here, though,' Lila said as she began the slow descent toward the farm house. 'Seems awfully isolated. Even a little scary.'

'Perhaps.'

The drive had nearly disappeared beneath weeds and thistles — surely more over-grown than merely the past few months would account for — so Lila turned most of her attention to picking her way around discarded bits of machinery, random-seeming piles of wood so weather-worn that it could serve no earthly purpose except as tinder, and assorted potholes and rocks that formed an unofficial minefield.

Neither she nor Ella spoke until the car stuttered to a stop a few yards from the porch. The engine clattered a couple of times after Lila had turned the ignition off, then with a shudder, died.

'So here we are,' Ella said into the silence. 'The old Stevenson place.'

'Yes. The last one.'

'Last?'

'I've gotten quit-signatures for all of the other farms in Shadow Valley. That's the last formal act of transferring ownership from the families to the government.'

'Ah, so that is what you are doing out here. I was wondering. You didn't look familiar and you certainly weren't familiar with the area. And it's not exactly the perfect place for a picnic.' There was an unspoken question in the casual comments, one that Lila chose not to answer.

'No,' she said, 'I'm not from here.'

They sat in silence for a while. A rather uncomfortable silence, if truth be told, because Lila really didn't want to discuss why she found herself at this derelict of a farm, and Ella seemed unwilling to introduce any new topics of conversation.

Finally, Ella broke the silence.

'Why are you out here?'

This time, faced with the direct questions, there was little Lila could easily do but respond. And truthfully, there was no reason not to.

'Here? Well . . . it's not quite the same situation as the other farms. I held off coming here until the end, until I had met with all of the other families. I had hoped that . . . '

'Yes.'

'Well, to be frank, I hoped to see someone out here. I would even have been glad . . . well, perhaps *relieved* would be a better word . . . to see an angry home-owner glowering at me from the porch. This silence . . . this emptiness . . . it's disconcerting.'

'So no one lives here?'

It seemed a bit odd to Lila that Ella, who obviously knew how to get to the Stevensons', didn't know what had happened. But before she could say anything about it, Ella continued. 'Why did you make the long trip, then, if there's no one here?'

'That's just the problem, Ella. I don't know if anyone lives out here or not.' Lila sighed. 'It's . . . it's complicated.' She felt like an actor in a badly scripted soap opera, falling back on triteness and cliché.

'I don't have anywhere to be in the next little while,' Ella said, fussing with a fleck of invisible dust on her blouse. That was an open invitation for Lila to tell all, even while the phrasing skirted any direct questions.

'Okay. Let's get out and check the front door. And I'll explain.'

They opened their doors and got out, their feet crackling on bits of dried grass and weeds. Together they made their way up three rather precarious steps, wobbling once or twice as the wooden risers threatened to give way, then stopped at the dark wooden door. Its panels were splintered and rough. Lila felt sorry for any hand that tried to knock on that surface.

The only thing breaking the unrelieved black of the wood was a small square of white paper covered with tiny print.

'That,' Lila said, pointing to the paper as if it were a source of lethal contamination, 'that is an Eminent Domain declaration.'

Ella looked at her blankly.

'That means that unless someone shows up today to sign for transferral of ownership, this house, the outbuildings, the land will all belong to the state government without any restitution to the current owner. The state gets it free. The owner gets screwed.'

'But I thought you said that no one lived here.'

'That's the problem. I don't know if anyone does or not.' Not for the first time today, Lila sighed deeply. She glanced around. At the far end of the porch an old wicker-work swing hung from two thick, rusted chains.

'That looks strong enough to support us,' she said. 'Let's sit down for a bit and I'll try to explain.'

The swing sagged slightly at the weight of the two women but gave no indication of giving up entirely. Ella brushed her foot lightly against the wooden porch, making the swing move slightly, as if it had caught an errant breeze.

'You know about the reservoir,' she began.

Ella nodded. 'I've heard bits and

pieces. Probably everyone in this part of the state has.'

'Well, the state — my boss, actually — wanted to make sure that everyone involved got fair treatment . . . as fair as possible, given that the reservoir was *going* to be built and the people here were *going* to have to leave . . . regardless. So about three months ago, once all of the details for constructing the reservoir were completed, he organized a meeting here in Shadow Valley. In the old church.'

'That would be before it was knocked down, of course,' Ella said with a faint smile.

'Uh . . . yes. A week or so before . . . Anyway, everyone in the Valley attended, mostly because final financial transactions were underway and my boss wanted to make sure there were no questions.'

'Were there any?'

That seemed like an odd response. Lila glanced at Ella, but the other woman was sitting in the swing, apparently relaxed, her foot still brushing the rough planks of the porch.

'A few. But really only one of any importance.'

'Yes,' Ella said when Lila seemed reluctant to continue. 'What was it?'

'It was whether or not the owner of this property would show up. Anna Stevenson. The last surviving member of her family.'

'And did she?'

Lila stood up and began pacing back and forth, her movements unconsciously parodying the slow rocking of the swing. To the porch rail turn, then back to the house, turn, to the porch rail, turn . . .

'No. Actually, she didn't. Most of the people there saw nothing unusual in that, though.'

She turned to face Ella.

'According to them, Anna Stevenson hadn't been seen outside of this house in over twenty years. Almost no one had even spoken to her in that time, except over the telephone she had installed just after she moved in. She was a recluse. Neighbours would leave supplies for her on this porch when she asked, and she always paid them for the supplies, with a bit extra for their taking the time to come all this way out.

'But they never saw her. Except perhaps as a movement, a shadow behind the curtains.'

Lila gestured to the two large front windows, actually noticing for the first time that — unlike the windows in so many of the houses she had visited recently, these were still closed off by draperies. The visible material was faded and stained, as if the drapes had been hanging in place for decades without being either opened or taken down for cleaning.

'So she didn't know about the plans for the reservoir?'

'Oh, she knew, all right. I even spoke to her once . . . by telephone. There was a bad connection, a great deal of static, so I had to hang up fairly soon, and we really didn't get to say much to each other, but she knew what was happening. She knew how much she would receive for her place . . . more than she would have gotten if she had tried to sell it, actually. Land values here in the Valley have dropped a lot over the past decade.'

Ella remained silent, swinging rhythmically back and forth. She turned to look out at the vista from the porch.

Lila followed her glance.

It was beautiful. Even weedy and overgrown, the land sloped gently downward from the house, offering a view of acres of land, mostly covered with scrub brush, with an occasional patch here and there that was probably some farmer's pasturage, or a field that in past years would have been nearing harvest time. On the other side of the valley, the mountains rose in a rough parapet, seeming to lean protectively over the intervening landscape.

'Perhaps she thought that beauty should count for something,' Ella said, with an edge to her voice that sounded as rough as the porch railing, splintered and worn. 'Perhaps she thought that history — that time and family and memory — were worth more than outsiders were offering.'

Lila stiffened. She had heard a similar tone in house after house over the past weeks. Usually it modulated rapidly into outright anger and indignation.

But Ella didn't live in Shadow Valley. She hadn't been at the meeting, nor did her name appear on any of the deeds Lila had examined.

'What . . . ' Lila started to say.

Behind her, one of the front windows shattered with a high, ringing *CRAAAK!*

4

Lila dropped to her knees. Her heart was racing but her breath seemed to have stopped entirely. She tried to make herself as small as possible, hunching behind one of the porch uprights.

When her ears stopped ringing, she forced herself to speak.

'Ella,' she whispered hoarsely. Her voice didn't sound like her own. 'Are you all right?'

She didn't dare move to look behind her.

'Yes,' Ella said. 'I'm fine. Are you?'

'Yes, I think so.' Lila had felt nothing. She didn't think she had been injured at all. But she was certain that she knew what had happened.

One of the farmers — most likely one she had met and talked with — had figured out where she still had to go, had followed her, and from the shelter of one of the clumps of wild rose had taken a shot at her.

And missed.

She told herself not to move. Not yet.

'Do you see anyone out there, Ella?'

Pause.

Silence.

Then: 'No, I don't think so. Do you think it is safe?'

Lila risked a glance over her shoulder. One of the panes in the nearest window was gone, leaving behind only ragged shards that looked dangerously sharp . . . *wicked sharp*, her grandmother might have said.

But the window itself was several feet away, closer to the center of the long porch span; and Lila and Ella had been together near the swing at the far end. She had not been near the window at all.

Surely anyone who was anything like a decent shot would have come closer if they wanted to do her . . . or Ella . . . harm.

Cautiously she straightened, then stood.

Nothing.

She heard the rustle of clothing behind her and turned to see Ella coming from around the back of the swing. Apparently she had taken refuge there as soon as she had heard the shot.

'Still nothing,' Ella said, peering over the top of the car. 'Whoever was there is either gone, or hasn't moved at all since . . . '

'But why now? Why here?' Lila took one step toward the broken window, then stopped.

There was no response from the shooter, wherever he . . . or she . . . might be.

'Still nothing?'

'No.' Ella sounded as if she had recovered from her fright. Her voice was low but steady. It made Lila feel slightly more courageous.

She bent low and reached for her briefcase, pulling it toward her from where she had dropped it. She knelt and opened it. Her cell phone was still in the leather case attached to the inside. She slipped it out and began punching numbers. She didn't have to look them up. By now she knew them from memory.

'Who are you calling?' Ella whispered.

'State police,' Lila said, depressing the final key.

One ring.

Two.

Then . . . static.

Nothing but static.

Lila stared at the phone, then hit the 'end call' button. She was certain that she had had sufficient bars to enable a call. She looked down at the cell. Three bars. Enough for a call. Not optimal, but enough.

She entered the telephone number again.

One ring.

Two.

Then . . . static.

'That's not possible!'

'What?'

Lila quickly explained what had happened, all the while ending the call, punching in the numbers once more, hearing the two rings . . . and then the static.

'It just did it again.'

'Cell service can be funny out here,' Ella said. 'Landlines, too. Something about the way the mountains jut up, some say. Or the minerals in some of the ridges.'

'But to ring twice, then cut out . . . '

Ella shrugged. 'Maybe it's like the car. If you try again later, you might get through. You never know out here.'

Lila looked at her but the other woman seemed serious. *Okay, we'll let the cell catch its breath and then dial again. Who knows?*

Aloud she said, 'I've called the office plenty of times from Shadow Valley and never had this happen.' But she slipped her cell into her pocket anyway and took another step toward the shattered window.

Glass fragments glittered in the weathered frame, winking at her in the afternoon light that filtered through the shadows on the porch. It looked as if the bottom of the frame was encased in diamonds . . . or at least in rhinestones. The light flickered bright and silvery against the dark background. Even the drapery lining seemed dark and solid against the dancing movement of the light.

'Wait a minute,' Lila said. She took yet another step toward the window. She was only two or three feet away.

Her feet crunched on something on the porch. Through the soles of her shoes, it felt like fine gravel, small and fragile but rough for all of that.

She looked down.

She was standing in a patch of glass . . . crushed, almost pulverized. She shifted her foot. The sound grated against the silence.

'That's not right.'

'What?' Ella said, coming closer and staring at the planks.

'That,' Lila said, pointing to the tiny fragments. 'That's from the window. But it's on the *outside*.'

'The outside?'

'Yes, and I'll bet . . . ' Oblivious to the fact that a minute before she had been cowering behind a wooden support, desperately hoping not to draw any more attention from the hidden shooter, she leaned forward and carefully thrust her hand through the empty frame. There were enough glass fragments still embedded in the decades-old putty to cut her fairly seriously if she drew her arm across them, but she had to find out.

She grasped the faded drapery lining — it felt like some sort of muslin, but stiff, either with accumulated dust and dirt or simply with age — and pulled it slowly to one side, exposing a smooth section perhaps eighteen inches across.

A *smooth* section.

She let the fabric drop and withdrew her hand.

'What?' Ella repeated.

'There should have been a bullet hole there,' Lila said. 'But there isn't. And the broken glass should have been *inside* the house, shouldn't it?'

She looked to Ella for confirmation but the older woman just stared at her.

'You know, if the bullet had struck the window, the glass should have fallen inside the house, not out here on the porch.' She knelt and gingerly picked up a few fragments. 'And I don't think it should be so thoroughly ground up. This looks like it's been blasted apart, not just broken by the impact of a bullet.'

'Let me see.'

Ella studied the glass Lila cradled in her palm.

'You know, I think you're right. This looks more like . . . well, like tiny gravel, or large grains of sand, than it does broken glass. And I know it wasn't on the porch when we walked by a few minutes ago.'

She didn't feel through the open pane as Lila had done but she did look closely at the fabric on the other side.

'And there *isn't* a bullet hole.'

'Maybe someone inside . . . '

'No,' Ella said. 'I didn't see any movement inside the whole time we were out here. And that wouldn't explain the glass.' She bore down with the toe of one shoe — square-toed, rather old-fashioned, Lila thought — and both of them heard the grating sound. 'No, that wouldn't explain this.'

'Maybe . . . ' Lila walked to the edge of the porch, shaded her eyes with one hand, and stared at the distant thicket of wild rose. 'Maybe . . . there wasn't a bullet.'

She turned, drew her cell phone from her pocket, and punched redial.

One ring.

Two.

Then static.

5

'What's going on here?' Lila's voice was tight with frustration, fury, and more than a tinge of fear. Her first impulse was to throw the cell as far from her as she could, send it hurtling into a distant patch of dying wild sunflowers and thick nettles where it would rest silently until the waters of Shadow Lake crept high enough to short its circuits and kill it forever.

After a moment's thought, however, she returned it to her pants pocket. *Give it a rest. Then maybe . . .*

Turning her attention from the cell to the other woman standing near her in the shade of the porch, she repeated, 'What's going on here? What in the name of all things holy is happening?'

Her vehemence seemed to startle Ella, who took a step backward but kept her eyes pinioned on Lila.

'Do *you* know anything about this?'

Even to Lila, it sounded as much an accusation as a question.

'I . . . uh . . . no, of course not. Wait, though . . . You said that the woman who lives . . . lived . . . here, Anna Stevenson, didn't come to your meeting. Maybe she's still around somewhere, maybe she was waiting for you to come this afternoon, and she . . . '

'And she what?' Lila broke in. She could feel her temper rising, overcoming both the frustration and the fear. 'Anna Stevenson *what?* *Magicked* a broken window? Because there isn't any sense pretending that this was done by a bullet. Nothing fits, neither a shooter out there' — Lila flung one hand toward the brightly lit front yard — 'nor one inside. You were right. I didn't see any movement in there, and I certainly don't hear anything now.'

'But if she . . . '

'Ella, that's the *real* problem.' Lila consciously forced herself to be calm . . . or at least calmer.

'What is?'

'No one knows if Anna Stevenson is

still living here or not. No one has heard from her — not by telephone, not by letter, not by note, not by freaking *carrier pigeon!* — since the night of the meeting. Three months, and not a single bit of evidence that the woman is here, that she is still alive. Nothing. That's really why I am out here.'

She took a deep breath — the air tasted warm, redolent with traces of dust and the acrid bitterness of sage from the surrounding hillsides — and physically squared her shoulders. Soldier preparing for battle. Let the fireworks begin.

'I have to go inside and verify that she has left . . . Somehow.'

'Go . . . *inside?*' Ella sounded nervous, unaccountably more nervous than when the two of them believed they had been targeted by a sniper.

'Yes, and post this.' Lila went back to her briefcase and pulled out a single piece of paper. 'Final notice. *Official* final notice. Then probably tomorrow or the next day or the next, out will come the bulldozers and down comes house, granary, sheds, ramshackle chicken coop, everything.'

As she spoke, her free hand reached to open the door.

'*Don't*,' Ella whispered as she grasped hold of Lila's arm and jerked back. 'Don't go in there. It might . . . it might not be . . . safe.' She glanced around, as if she expected to see a dark shadow lurking at the end of the porch or an ethereal hand emerging through the empty pane barely feet from them.

Lila shook off Ella's hand, but she made no further attempt to open the door.

'Ella, tell me the truth. Do you know something about this place, about Anna Stevenson, that you aren't telling me?'

'No, not really. It's just . . . it's just that . . . ' She was nearly in tears. Even in the filtered light, Lila could see that.

'Please, Ella?'

'I can't tell you anything specific. Like I said, I grew up on another farm, a ways from here.' Again she gestured back toward the core of Shadow Valley. 'I never came out here as a child. I don't know of anyone who ever did. None of the kids, anyway.

'But when we were together, just us kids, without any adults around, we would whisper stories about the . . . the *haunted house*.' She giggled — the sound echoed across the porch and made Lila feel uncomfortable. Somehow it didn't fit. Neither the right time nor the right place.

'Oh, I suppose that as we grew older, we knew deep down that we were just telling tales, that there wasn't really anything haunted about the place. But back then, the stories seemed *real*. Bits and pieces we had gleaned from overhearing our parents talking about the Stevensons.

'People *died* out here, long ago. That much was real, although none of us knew the details and our parents wouldn't talk about it, not even as we grew older and began asking more serious questions.'

Ella shuddered.

'And all that time, no one we knew ever *saw* the woman who lived here, an 'old maid', we would have called her, named Annie . . . not the Anna who lives here now, but an older relative. Then the old woman died and . . . I moved away.'

'But . . . '

'I know, none of this makes any sense, maybe in the world of fantasy and childish make-believe all of the pieces would fit together, but not in the real world. So, truly, I can't tell you anything more. Except that I don't think it is a good idea for you to go inside this house.'

Ella took one more step back.

Lila hadn't moved since Ella had begun talking. She simply stood there, listening, barely breathing.

Haunted house? Mysterious old woman?

No one she had talked to thus far had mentioned anything like this. As far as Lila knew from her spotty conversations with the farmers and their families, the Stevenson place was just another time-worn homestead, one that had long since outlived its usefulness and, like the rest of them, was about to be submerged beneath the silent waters of the reservoir.

She shook herself, as if she were waking from a bad dream.

'Ella, you know that those were only stories the other kids must have made up to explain a lonely, difficult old woman.

Stories like that happen all of the time. In another age, in another place, they might have gotten old Annie Stevenson burned as a witch, but . . . '

'I know. But old stories are hard to forget. And seeing you with your hand reaching out . . . I . . . oh, forget it,' she finished, flashing her wide smile. 'I'm sorry I interrupted you. You know what you have to do, and here I am wasting your time with old wives' tales. Well, old children's tales, perhaps, but you know what I mean.'

Even so, Ella did not come any closer to the door.

Lila had made up her mind, however. There had been no shooter, no bullet speeding past them to bury itself . . . somewhere. There was no danger. The window was obviously old, ancient almost. Even where she stood she could see that the remaining panes in the old frames were rippled, wavy with age and time, and that they might easily shatter at the slightest touch. Probably a bit of wind striking the glass at the wrong angle. A momentary settling of the house's unstable foundations. Something like that. And, *voilà*, broken window.

She straightened again and stepped toward the door, holding out her hand to turn the knob. She was pleased to see that her hand was not shaking.

She had not quite touched the metal — she could still see a thin sliver of light between her fingers and the dully gleaming brass knob — when . . .

Craaaack!

With a shattering sound as ear-splitting as the first had been, one of the panes in the window on the *other* side of the door burst, then tumbled in a cascade of fragments barely larger than dust to the porch.

Ella let out a little shriek as she jumped back several paces.

Lila froze, then spun on her heels and stalked toward the car.

'That's it! I've had it!'

Hugging her briefcase tight against her chest, as if it were some mystical, impervious armor, she clattered down the steps, for all intents oblivious to even the possibility of a sniper. She yanked

51

open the door of the car. The handle was burning hot from sitting in the late afternoon sun but she ignored the pain.

'Come on, Ella,' she called over her shoulder, 'We're getting out of here. Now. I don't care if it's disappearing bullets or self-destructive window panes, or magic from the depths of time and space, or little green men from Mars . . . I'm not sticking around here to find out. It's not in my job description.'

By then she had tossed her briefcase into the back seat, dropped into the driver's seat, and, without bothering to buckle up, jammed the key into the ignition.

When she glanced sideways at the farm house, Ella had not moved from the porch. She had not moved at all. The look on her face suggested that she couldn't quite believe Lila's reaction to the breaking glass. Or that she was more wary of Lila than of any shenanigans the house might wish to pull.

Leave her, then. She had her chance. She probably has a car around here somewhere anyway. She can handle things for herself.

Almost savagely, Lila twisted the key.

The engine turned over once.

Coughed.

Shuddered like a fatally-stricken man in the final stages of convulsions.

Died.

She cranked the ignition a second time.

Nothing. Dead silence. Not even the *click-click-click* of a worn-out alternator or a powerless battery.

She started to say something. Stopped. Then simply rested her head on her hands, still gripping the steering wheel. Under her breath, she counted to ten.

Then to ten again.

And again.

Finally she leaned back, sighed resignedly, gently removed the key from the ignition, and trudged back up the steps to face the door.

'All right. I give up. No cell calls. No car to get us out of here. I suppose if we tried to walk out, we would find the end of the driveway hedged up by brambles, like Sleeping Beauty's palace, or overrun by rattlesnakes hissing and spitting and coiled to strike.

'We apparently can't leave. We can't call for help.

'So I'm going in. You with me, Ella?'

6

Ella still hadn't moved. To all appearances, she hadn't even breathed since the second window blew, although Lila knew that if that had been the case, the older woman would be lying senseless on the porch.

Lila passed her and stepped again — *third time's the charm* — to the door. She paused just before her foot touched the threshold. She wondered momentarily how many feet had crossed over that worn and stained slab of heavily grained oak, how many others had gained entry to this house . . . and how many had been refused.

She spoke to Ella again, not turning her head.

'Are you coming?'

'I . . . I suppose I had better. Although I still don't think . . . '

'I may agree with you, but I don't think we have an option. Not unless you want to walk three or four miles back to Shadow Valley, with twilight coming on, and no hope of finding anyone home when we get back there.'

Apparently she spoke for Ella as well as for herself. She felt a tenuous grip on her arm, not intended this time to pull her back but rather to offer faint but hopeful support. As she stood before the door, she felt Ella's hand cease trembling.

'All right, then. Here we go.'

She stretched out her hand, fingers extended, hesitant.

Nothing happened.

Without a word passing between them, she and Ella glanced at the windows on each side of the doorway, half-expecting the panes to explode onto the porch.

Nothing.

She took a deep breath and . . . touched the door knob.

Nothing.

The knob felt neither hot nor cold, just as warm as it should on a summer's afternoon. Nothing spooky there.

She turned it slowly.

The mechanism worked smoothly and

silently. There had been a reasonable chance, she realized, that the door would have been locked, especially since the owner hadn't been heard from for months. For all she knew, delegations of families had been out here to check up on things, and certainly one of them would have locked the door behind them.

No, if Ella was right, the last thing on anyone's mind in Shadow Valley — except my own — would be housebreaking at the Haunted Mansion.

The door swung easily open, revealing a long, dark hallway, paneled on either side with dark, almost black wainscoting. Other than the faint sunlight filtering over her shoulder, she could see no illumination in the house at all. Just abysmal darkness that extended seemingly forever.

'Great,' she whispered half to herself. 'No lights.'

But then, she hadn't actually expected any. No electricity at any rate. Power to Shadow Valley had been cut off several days ago, when the last of the families packed their remaining goods in a battered, decades-old picket-sided truck and trundled their way up the highway leading out of the valley. Lila had seen the rep from the electric company flick a switch at the main junction box, up where the parking lot for the church had been. So, no electricity.

Still, in the back of her mind, she had probably anticipated the same dust-shafted slants of light coming through dirty, undraped windows that she had seen elsewhere in the valley, but apparently the architecture of the Stevenson place was different. Access to any windows from the hallway was apparently impossible.

Behind her, Ella gave her a slight nudge.

Now that the last barricade protecting the Wicked Queen's castle had been breached — now that the door had been safely opened — Ella's reticence about entering had obviously been replaced by curiosity, however hesitant.

Lila stepped inside. Ella followed so closely that she could have been Lila's shadow rather than a separate entity.

The house was absolutely silent.

Dead-seeming. No rustles, no creaks, no tiny pattering of even tinier feet — rats, mice, lizards, whatever might have entered during the owner's absence. But there was a . . . a . . .

'Do you smell that?' Lila spoke in an even quieter whisper than before, as if afraid to waken someone — *something* — residing in the depths of the darkness. 'Is that . . . ?'

Ella gave a small sniff. Then another.

'Yes, I think so.'

'Chocolate?' Lila asked herself as much as she was asking Ella. The scent was faded and hazy, tenuous, but nonetheless present.

'Chocolate,' Ella affirmed, with a final sniff. 'Definitely chocolate.'

The house should have smelled of dust and mold and age and disuse. Lila had been in sufficient numbers of such places to know what to expect.

But *chocolate*?

Her mind was so busy trying to sort out the impossible report being communicated to her brain by one of her senses that she didn't consciously notice her hand reaching out to touch the darkened wall, at just the spot one would expect to find a light switch.

Nor did she register the fact of her finger flipping the switch upward, to the 'on' position.

She did, however, respond with a small cry and a short step backward — inadvertently treading on Ella's toes, so close was the other woman to her — to the sudden, utterly unexpected glow of a single light bulb depending from an antique-looking fixture in the middle of the hallway.

'Oh, my,' Ella breathed, as stunned as Lila.

'But . . . but that's *impossible*,' Lila said. 'There isn't . . . there *can't* be . . . '

But there was.

As if to test her unbelief, Lila flipped another switch. Up ahead, from a sconce on the wall near a dark staircase, a second light glowed. She tried a third switch. This time the glow came from the top of the staircase, revealing a portion of hallway paneled in what looked to be identical dark wood.

By this time, both women had stepped far enough into the main hall to see that on both sides, sets of tall, wide, polished pocket doors were built into the walls. The doors looked to be identical.

Behind them, the front door swung quietly to, the mechanism catching with an audible *snick*.

Ella yelped and turned to try the knob.

'At least that's something,' she said after a moment. 'It's not locked. We can get out of this place whenever we want.'

But Lila did not want to.

Even though her briefcase still sat in a patch of sunlight on the back seat of her rental, still containing all of the papers relating to the Stevenson place, Lila did not want to leave, not even long enough to retrieve her official justification for being there.

It was as if the house *called* to her.

Nonsense, she thought. *That's ridiculous. It's just an interesting old place, that's all, a farm house like all of the others, with a rather atypical design, perhaps, but just an old house after all.*

Yes, came an answering voice, one she

61

didn't quite recognize, *with exploding windows and impossible electricity. Just a regular, run-of-the-farm old house.*

'Lila, look at this!'

Ella's voice tore Lila from her trance.

The other woman was standing next to the pocket doors on the left-hand wall. One of them had slid back two or three inches.

'There is a lock here, but the door opened anyway.' She pushed on the panel, then on the other one, until they stood a yard apart, wide open enough for the women to see into the room.

Into the *parlour.*

Because that was undoubtedly the room's purpose. Enough light spilled through the doorway from the hall for them to see the rounded curves of an old-fashioned settee — Lila would have been willing to bet anything, to *bet the farm*, that it was upholstered in deep crimson velvet . . . or what would have to pass for deep crimson after years of use. An end-table stood at one side. Both sat only a few feet from the front window, heavily curtained in material so thick that no light seeped through from the outside. Even though both of the women knew that a broken pane lay hidden on the other side, neither could see the slightest hint of movement in the draperies.

Ella stepped inside and, as Lila had done in the hall, reached out to where a light switch should be. Lila heard the *click* and saw the multi-armed chandelier in the center of the ceiling flicker into life.

She had been right. The sofa — and the curtains — *had* been a deep wine color, faded now to a hideous red-grey-brown, almost like dusty, crusted blood. *Puce*, possibly, Lila thought, knowing the word but never actually having seen anything that pretended to the grandeur of such an exotic name.

Or such an ugly name.

The wooden parts of the sofa, and the end-table, looked to be mahogany, dark and secretive and old. Everything in the room looked old, although there wasn't much. A footstool in front of the sofa, almost touching where the heavy curtains pooled on the worn, dark floral design of an old carpet. A single bookshelf containing no more than a dozen books along the far wall. A small desk and matching chair on the wall opposite the window. A fireplace that looked as if it hadn't been cleaned since the invention of the electric bulb, to judge from the accumulation of soot and dust on the hearth and on the painted bricks that surrounded its open maw.

That was it.

Even though the room could easily have held twice the number of pieces — and during Victorian times perhaps three or four times as many, given the period's penchant for creating dark labyrinthine interiors, that was all.

It gave Lila a sudden chill.

She stepped into the parlour and walked slowly around, running her fingers along the stiff velvet nap of the sofa, touching the top of the end-table with as much care as if it had been as fragile as a soap bubble.

From there she moved to the single bookcase, also in age-darkened mahogany, standing nearly to her shoulders but empty save for a handful of books on the top shelf and a single volume lying on its side on the second.

She glanced at the upright titles. An ancient bible, its black leather spine pitted and torn by use, the gilt of its title nearly rubbed away, leaving little more than the ghostly imprint of nine capital letters. Several more volumes, also bound in black or brown leather, so old that nothing remained of their titles. She felt an odd reluctance to touch them. The last book, canting against the others as if too weak to carry on the struggle against gravity on its own, was thinner than the others, bound in what appeared to be a faded floral brocade. *Tender Thoughts: Verses* was just legible on the spine. Lila could imagine the kind of poetry that might rest between the covers. Saccharine, maudlin, or both. It did not appeal to her.

She dropped her gaze to the single book on the second shelf.

The cover was dusty, smudged, almost unreadable, but enough remained of the gilt title for her to make out the word

Journal impressed in unduly ornate letters onto the brown leather.

Journal.

Whose?

She had raised her hand to pick up the book when a thought intruded. She turned around, ready to ask Ella . . .

But the question never came.

Ella was not there.

The parlor was empty, save for Lila and the scattering of furniture.

There was not even a second set of footprints in the light dust obscuring portions of the carpet.

'Ella? Ella, where are you?'

Lila crossed the room and entered the hall. She tried the pocket doors on the opposite wall but they were firmly locked. No amount of pulling or pushing moved them at all. So. Ella hadn't gone into the second room to explore.

Lila continued down the hall until stopped, just past the stairway, by another door, this one hinged to open outward . . . and this one locked as tightly as the pocket doors.

'Ella? Answer me, Ella. Where are you?'

Lila stopped to listen intently.

There was no response. There were no sounds of an answering call. And no light *click-click-click* of shoes on hardwood flooring, neither downstairs — where it was obvious that Lila was alone — nor echoing from upstairs.

Turning, she made her way back to the front door. Perhaps Ella had been overcome by the dust, or spooked by the silence. Perhaps she had stepped outside for a breath of clean air.

Lila opened the door.

To her surprise, the afternoon sun seemed to be resting on the crest of the distant mountains. The shadows criss-crossing the yard already had the misty tinge of twilight.

And yet they — *she* — had only been inside for a few moments. Out here, it was as if hours had passed. She could almost see the sun sinking as she stood there.

'Ella!' Her voice was tinged with concern, even with fear. 'Ella!'

Suddenly she remembered her cell phone, snug in her pocket. She retrieved it and punched redial yet again.

Two rings.

Static.

Just as before.

'Ella! I hope you aren't playing some kind of game with me. Please answer me. Are you out here? Ella!'

The only response was a faint, half-hearted echo, *la-la-la*, that faded too soon into silence.

Lila took the ramshackle steps in two strides, and in two more was beside her car. She yanked the front door open — the handle was cooler now, almost clammy — and slid onto the driver's seat. She inserted the key, said a silent prayer, and turned.

Nothing.

Not even a *click* to tell her that there was life somewhere in the engine.

She got out again.

The disk of the sun was now partially obscured by the mountains. It was getting darker rapidly.

She punched the redial button on her cell again, more from anger, fear, and frustration than from any hope that her call would get through.

Nothing. Not even the two initial rings that she half-expected. Not even any static.

'Ella!' This time there was no missing the quaver of fear in her voice. 'Ella, answer me!'

She shivered.

She looked over the top of the car at the wild-rose thickets that would lead her back to the road and from there back to Shadow Valley proper.

They were in full shadow . . . and to her imagination, the shadows seemed to shift and move as if alive.

No, she couldn't walk between those thorny barricades, alone, at night, in an unfamiliar place. Anything would be better than that.

The car, then. Safely ensconced inside with the doors securely locked and the windows up.

Okay, she could justify not walking out of here by herself. But somehow she just couldn't stomach the idea of hiding away in the car, terrified by every sound, by the high-pitched wail of a distant coyote or the scrape of a twig, caught up in the wind and dragged across the roof.

The house, then.

At least she could lock the front door from the inside, and the shattered panes were probably too small for anyone to crawl through.

What am I doing, she thought. *Preparing for war?*

Yes, the same half-familiar voice responded. *Yes, you are.*

7

Once inside the house, her back pressed against the front door she had carefully closed and locked, Lila paused to take stock.

'Now what?' She spoke out loud, even though her voice sounded strange, almost alien, in the utter silence. Not to speak would have made her feel even more uncomfortable, as if the dark walls and glowering ceiling were pressing in on her.

'Now what?'

First — check out the rest of the house. Thus far, she and Ella — *where was Ella? what had happened to her?* — had only entered one room, the parlor. What about the other rooms, especially the ones upstairs?

She stepped over to the pocket doors on the right-hand wall. The ones that were locked.

This time, she paid close attention as she grasped the handles and pulled, first gently then with increasing force.

Something was wrong.

It took a moment or two for her to figure out what. Usually, when someone tugged at a locked door, there was some movement, however fractional, as the mechanism shifted. The door might jiggle ever so slightly. The lock might tick against its metal casing.

But here, there was nothing. No movement at all. It was as if the two doors were actually a single piece of wood, decorated with Trompe-l'œil designed to create the *illusion* of pocket doors, including deep shadows where the panels would, theoretically at least, slide into the walls on both sides.

Carefully Lila ran her thumbnail up the slit that should have marked where the two panels met, testing to see if she could insinuate her nail any deeper into the crack. But no, it was as if even the slight indentation was part of a master plan to fool, to confound.

There was no movement at all.

Sighing, she turned and crossed the hall to stand in the entry to the parlor.

Nothing had changed there. The furniture was as it had been. The light still glowed in the overhead chandelier, casting shadows in the corners and beneath the scattered pieces. She had half expected to see Ella sitting on the sofa, waiting for her to return, but there was no one in the room.

That left the door at the end of the hall and whatever might await her upstairs.

Stopping only to reassure herself that the front door was securely locked, even giving the knob a quick shake and feeling the door shift slightly with the pressure, she made her way down the hall.

The dark wood of the paneling was even more oppressive-seeming now than it had been before. For the first time, Lila registered the fact that there were no paintings on the walls, no family portraits, not even any cutouts from the annual calendars provided by the local feed stores. A number of the other houses had had landscapes — or fashion-photographs of calves, ducks, and horses — thumb-tacked to the walls in lieu of more expensive art.

Here, nothing.

She reached the door at the far end, and tried to open it. Before, she had only noted that the door was locked; now, she could feel that, as with the pocket doors, there was no give to the door at all. It might as well be part of the wall, cunningly painted to pass for an entry-way. She even squatted down to check for any tell-tale bit of light that might seep under the door.

Nothing there, either.

'Curiouser and curiouser.' Now her voice startled her. The surrounding woodwork seemed to absorb the vitality, echoing back only a thin, dead mockery of her usually rich contralto. Perhaps it would be best not to say anything more out loud.

She moved back down the hall to stand at the foot of the stairway. The treads were bare, as was the hall floor, composed of oak planks that showed signs of decades of wear. Still, they were at least polished and, as far as she could see, splinter-free.

She glanced upwards.

The single light at the top of the stairway provided enough light for her to see the steps clearly but little beyond that. Whatever lay upstairs was shrouded in mystery and darkness.

She half decided to return to the parlour and wait there until . . .

Until what?

Until Ella returned . . . from wherever she was?

Until darkness lifted and the sun shone again on the bramble-choked lane that led back to Shadow Valley?

Until . . . until the silent, black water of the reservoir rose, inevitable and unstoppable, until it swallowed her car, the porch, the house itself . . . and her?

No, that was not right. She had to keep looking, try to find out what was happening around her.

She placed one foot on the lowest tread.

She had expected a *squeak*, a *crack* of old wood giving slightly under the pressure of her foot.

Nothing.

She was getting used to that. The house

seemed built on nothing. No sound, no movement.

She took another step. Another.

Silently, she ascended toward the second story.

Below, all remained quiet and still.

From the top of the stairs, the upper hall stretched empty and still, dimly lit by the single sconce on the wall beside her. At both ends were windows, but either it was too dark outside to see anything, or they were too grimed over with dust to be more than slightly translucent. At any rate, no light came from either.

The passageway was as devoid of ornamentation as had been the rooms below — nothing marred the blank stretches of dark paneling except for six doors, three on each side, set into the walls. There was no indication of light behind any of the doors; either there was none, or the doors fit their frames too tightly for any to escape through cracks.

Lila was fairly sure that the former alternative was the true one.

She tried the nearest door, the last one on the left-hand wall.

As she had expected, the knob did not move. The door did not rattle in its frame. It was as if it were a solid extension of the wall surrounding it.

She continued up the hallway, trying each of the other two doors. The second was locked as tightly as the first. So was the third, except that, standing close to it and putting her ear next to the panel — not *against* it, no, not quite, but as close as possible without actually touching it — she thought she heard . . . or felt . . . a kind of whispering static, a rise and fall of white noise so faint that it might have originated inside her own head rather than from behind the door.

Except she hadn't heard anything outside the other two.

Tentatively, she laid her palm against the door panel, fingers extended, and concentrated.

Almost, *almost*, she thought she felt a small vibration, not as if the door was any less securely locked than the others she had felt, but as if something were moving inside, slipping on silent currents of air just enough to register a presence.

'Hello,' she said. 'Is anyone in there? Ella?'

There was no answer. And the vibrations — if indeed there had been any — seemed to cease.

She backed away from the door, walking slowly and silently, until she felt the opposite wall. Turning, she tried the first door — the one that should open onto a room directly above the parlor below.

And the next.

And the next.

As she had anticipated, there was no sound within any of them, the door knobs were as unmoving as if carved of granite, and the doors refused even to vibrate as she pushed against them.

Since she again stood at the end of the hall nearest the stairs, she took a moment to glance out of the window.

Solid blackness met her eyes, as if the exterior of the pane had been painted black. She touched the glass. It was neither warm nor cold. She tried to push the frame up from the jamb but it would not move at all. It felt as if it had been nailed in place.

Probably the other window was exactly the same.

Shaking her head slightly, she retreated to the stairway and descended, back down to the main hall.

Nothing had changed.

She walked the length of the hall and turned into the only open doors — apparently — in the entire house. The parlor was, again, untouched from when she had looked at it before.

She entered, turned full circle in the center of the room, mostly to examine all of the shadowy corners, and then stood as still as death, immediately beneath the chandelier.

What now?

She turned again, more slowly. The bookcase caught her attention, for no reason other than that it was the only piece of furniture along the far wall.

She crossed over to it and held her hand out, not quite touching the spines on the upper shelf.

Not the Bible, she told herself. It didn't seem right. Silently she eliminated each of the other books standing upright on the shelf, shuddering slightly when her fingertips passed over the spine of *Tender Thoughts: Verses.*

Definitely not that one.

She settled for the solitary volume on the second shelf, the journal. When she picked it up, she could see clearly where it had been, its shape bordered by a thick layer of dust. Apparently the book hadn't been moved in months . . . perhaps years.

Yet she didn't feel at all guilty or intrusive as she carried it over to the velvet sofa, dusting the cover with the sleeve of her blouse.

She sat down. The overhead chandelier cast just enough light — and from the perfect angle — for her to read the cover easily, even though the words were faded and, in spite of her efforts, grainy with dust. Apparently the sofa had been placed with two ideals in mind — a view of the sunset out the front window (or at least a possible view, since with the drapes drawn, Lila couldn't be sure of what she would see) and a place to relax and read.

Even though there were precious few books to be seen.

She leaned back into the velvet pile, feeling its roughness and brittleness through the material of her blouse.

She opened the cover of the journal.

Words began immediately at the top of the first page. There was no introduction, no 'This journal belongs to' inscribed anywhere on either the first page or the flyleaf. The handwriting was clear and easily readable, although faded by time. It looked as if the entry had been written in black ink with an old-fashioned pen — the nib had apparently caught here and there on the texture of the rough paper, scattering tiny droplets of black across some of the letters.

It looked as though the words had been written in haste — carefully, to be sure, but rapidly as well.

She settled back and began to read.

8

I don't know if I can do this. But I *do* know that I have to try. Too much depends on it, not the least of which is my sanity.

Because I am *not* insane. I'm sure of that at least, even if nothing else makes much sense.

I know that I can't talk to anyone else about what has happened. I've been warned and I understand completely what that means. Oh, believe me, I understand.

But I have to make certain that I am not the only one who knows. That means writing it down, even though I am not a very good writer. Words don't flow from my pen. They stumble and meander and occasionally wobble before they find the strength to stand upright under their own power. So I hope that I can do this right.

I read somewhere, in a novel, I think, that the best place to begin is with the *place*. To understand the people, you have to understand the landscape that helped form them. In this case, the landscape is crucial. I don't think the things I'm about to write could happen anywhere else. At least, I hope and pray that they can't.

So, begin with the place.

Here goes . . .

★   ★   ★

Most people don't even know this place exists. The few who do call it Shadow Valley, although the name appears on no maps, on no county or state registers. It is less a town or a village than a ragged patchwork of farmhouses set a quarter-mile or so apart. Half a dozen or so line a gravel road most of the locals laughingly call 'Main Street.' Main Street begins nowhere and ends nowhere. That says a good deal about Shadow Valley.

It hunkers in a wide hollow, ten miles beyond the monument at Point of the Mountains that commemorates the last

Indian massacre of white settlers in the state. In the spring the valley assumes a green veneer of prettiness that occasionally fools passing motorists. Feathery grey-green poplars along irrigation ditches contrast with the variegated greens and golds of corn and wheat and scattered truck gardens. For a short time, the valley can look pretty.

But in January, everything is different.

In January, winds whistle through Black Willow Canyon, freezing, biting winds straight off the year-round snowcap of Mount Cleveland. They rip through bare upraised arms of emaciated poplars and gnarled box elders, and whirl across empty fields scored with skeletal stubble and clots of frozen earth the color of dried blood.

When there is snow, the valley attains a starkly forbidding picturesqueness. At the right time of day, that is, and from far enough away.

But when Aunt Annie died, the valley hadn't seen that much snow for over twenty years. Old man Willard's four-horse sleigh, large enough to carry fifteen merrymakers through drifts higher than their heads, hadn't moved an inch for three decades. It sat in its own ruts, shrouded in dust and decaying leaves and the acrid whiteness of bird droppings. Its wooden runners had warped away from the rusty pins that should have held them in place.

Travellers mostly don't even know they have been through Shadow Valley until they get to Oak Park on the other end of the county road. They swing around Point of the Mountain, past the historical marker telling about the Great Uprising of 1895, then follow the two-lane blacktop into the valley. They might notice the old Tuttle place off to the left, its sod roof crumbling between weathered silvery posts. Or the graveyard perched on the slope like a discolored patch of lichen, faded and barren against the sagebrush. They pass the old abandoned schoolhouse crouching behind its thorny barricade of hip-high weeds. Sometimes they notice Tower Rock thrusting up on the northern crest of the mountains that enclose the valley. Most times they don't.

They never even come close to the old house set way back from the rough track that heads east from the point where Main Street ends. The house squats at the end of a driveway so overgrown and faded it can't remember when it last felt tires. You can't see it from the county road two or three miles to the north.

That house is Aunt Annie's place. Travellers don't know about her. They wouldn't want to.

Aunt Annie wasn't my aunt, not really. She was a sort of shirt-tail great aunt, actually, my grandmother's half-sister. There wasn't much family left in Shadow Valley when I got the letter about Aunt Annie. Only my cousin Anna, named through some horrible mischance after Aunt Annie.

I didn't make it to the funeral. Only later in the summer, when the searing heat had baked the valley dry and the air hung heavy over dried-up corn and wheat that looked nearly dead, could I get back to Shadow Valley.

I wish to God now that I hadn't.

Aunt Annie seemed unutterably old

86

when she finally died.

She had lived alone since her mother burned to death in a kitchen fire in 1914. The house, battered by the years of weather and neglect, stood forlornly on one of the original homesteads. Two stories of hand-cut pine Aunt Annie's father had pulled down from Mount Cleveland by horse team to build a home for his wives.

Yes, wives. Four of them.

But only two in Shadow Valley. The other two lived up north in Canada. They had moved there long before the government in D.C. made it a crime to practice polygamy. Grandma told stories about her father's six-month trips to Aunt Naomi and Aunt Ethel. It was years before I understood what she wasn't coming right out and saying. Grandma wasn't exactly ashamed about her family. She just didn't like to talk about it.

Aunt Annie, now, she was different.

She hated her father and she hated all three of her father's other wives. Her mother had been the last, a young woman, beautiful by all accounts. I suppose you can't believe the lithograph of her hanging in its dark oak frame over the fireplace in the parlor. Nobody, it seems, ever walked away from an encounter with a lithographer looking like anything but a sour old witch.

Now, to be fair, Great-granddad had tried to do right by all four of his families. The two wives in Canada each had a place of her own on farms separated by a measly little creek that dried up by April of each year. But the houses were separate.

By the time he settled in Shadow Valley, though, things were different. By then, Great-granddad couldn't quite swing two places. So he compromised, like many of the old-time polygamists did.

He built two houses under one roof.

The place had two full kitchens. One has long since been turned into a pantry. Upstairs were two sets of bedrooms — six in all, three on each side of a hallway originally partitioned to make the bedrooms seem like two apartments. The partitions came down long ago, too.

And there were two front parlours.

Aunt Mattie, the first wife, insisted on that. The two other wives in Canada were all right with her, she is supposed to have said when Great-granddad began roughing out plans for the house on the Shadow Valley homestead, but no other woman would ever tell her what to do in her own parlour. So even before Aunt Annie's mother officially became part of the family, Great-granddad built the house with two parlours on the ground floor.

Aunt Mattie filled up her allotment of bedrooms easily, with my grandma and her two sisters in one, four brothers in the other. Mattie's side of the house was lively, if Grandma's stories can be trusted.

The other side was much, much quieter.

There was only one child. Annie. There had been others, but they were all born dead. One was stillborn, one had the umbilical cord cinched so tightly around his neck that it nearly cut through the tender flesh. Family gossip, not yet stilled by the passing years, also whispered of hideous deformities.

At any rate, there was 'Aunt' Rachel, alone in spite of the growing crowds around her. I remember Grandma telling me about Rachel sitting hour after hour in her parlour, Annie playing quietly with a box of old buttons and a needle and a string with no knot at the end. It curled like a snake back into the button box, and almost as quickly as the large, hand-carved buttons slipped onto her string they fell again into the pile at the bottom of the box. Annie never seemed to notice that she was making no progress at all.

Rachel hated everything about her life. Everything except Annie. The baby received all of the love the woman had to offer. Maybe too much of it.

And Rachel always complained, mostly about not having things. By the time Grandma could remember clearly (she was Mattie's youngest, born about three years after Rachel finally delivered a living child), Great-granddad was having a rough time. He had to quit his trips to Canada. He had no money for them any more, and besides, the kids up there were almost fully-grown. He sold both farm-houses eventually. I don't know what happened to the wives and kids.

But with eight youngsters still in Shadow Valley, he was pressed to find the where-withal to care for them. Grandma told stories of sparse winters and cold nights when the three girls would huddle together beneath a single worn quilt. Their teeth would chatter as loudly as the screaming wind and snow outside.

Aunt Rachel, of course, had only one child to care for, so she got less than Aunt Mattie. Much less than she felt she deserved. She had her parlor, her kitchen, her suite of empty bedrooms so cold that beards of ice caked the windows in the dead of winter. Two of the rooms were vacant, since Annie always slept in her mother's bed. Mattie envied those two empty rooms whenever she saw her four boys cramped into a room barely large enough for two, but she never mentioned them to Rachel. Rachel guarded the rooms with the acquisitiveness a dragon feels for its hoard.

But Rachel believed to the bottom of

her heart that she deserved more.

She took her bitterness out on the others. Great-granddad died in 1910 when a horse-drawn plow skittered over the frozen earth one day in early spring and sliced him open from throat to groin. Rachel had warned him that the ground was too hard. As he stomped out the kitchen door, she stared at him with an expression the rest of the family grew to understand, to hate . . . and to fear. She had warned him but he wouldn't listen.

Over the years she warned others as well, about many things. The lucky ones listened.

Edmond went next, less than a month after his father's burial. In those years before inoculations and adequate medical treatment, *diphtheria* was a word that struck dread into every mother's heart. Grandma told me once about watching her brother choke to death on a cot in the kitchen, his face twisted in agony, his throat grey and dead-looking even before the last of life left his body. Rachel had warned him about going fishing with Joe Miller, the neighbor boy who showed the first signs of the disease the night they came home with the first catch of the year. Joe Miller was dead three days later. Edmond lasted a week.

And then he was dead, too.

Albert went that summer. At twenty-four, he suddenly had to assume the mantle of eldest son and man of the house. He took his responsibilities seriously. One day in early June, he hitched the team to the wagon, sharpened his axe, and headed into the ranges below Mount Cleveland to cut wood for winter. Rachel warned him not to go alone. She warned him about rattlers and rocky trails and trees that fell the wrong way and sharp axes that sometimes willfully severed human flesh instead of timber.

She warned him.

The team returned just after supper that night. The buckboard wagon was half full of cut ash — it made the hottest fires, Albert knew. The search parties didn't find Albert's crushed remains for a week. By that time, there was little left of his face and hands and feet, and the flesh along his rib cage had been ripped off in ragged strips — but there was enough left to see the hideous gash that had nearly severed his right leg, and the bloodstained axe lying next to the body in a pool of crusted brown that was Albert's blood.

Rachel nodded once when she heard the news. She had warned him.

Aunt Mattie was pretty old by that time, a good twenty years older than Rachel. For a while, she tried to keep the farm going, but she didn't have the heart for it. Finally, she just picked up and left. She moved herself and what was left of her family down the road to Oak Park where she had folks. Somehow, Rachel found the money to buy the place from Mattie, money from her family maybe, although no one knew where she came from or who her folks were. The money was there, though, right to the dollar to meet the price Mattie had put on the house, the farm, the animals. Rachel paid, and Mattie left.

None of Mattie's kids came back to Shadow Valley except Grandma, when she got married.

The move left Rachel alone with the

house . . . and with Annie.

She locked up most of the rooms the way they were on the day Mattie left. No one I know ever went into the bedrooms on Mattie's side of the house until the day Aunt Annie died. Rachel took over Mattie's parlor. Oh yes, she moved her heavy Victorian plush couch in front of the north window (she had always coveted that window) and spent hours watching the sunsets in the summer. She re-arranged her furniture throughout the ground floor; she even sent away to Chicago and New York for new pieces, things that Great-Grandpa had not allowed her to buy.

I suppose she was finally happy.

And every February 14th, the postman hand-delivered a one-pound box of chocolates.

At first they came by special carriage from Burlington, the nearest town of any size. Most of the people in Shadow Valley figured that Rachel sent them herself. After what she considered years of neglect, she must have needed something tangible to prove something to herself, so every February 14th there came a gaudy box, stiff with ribbons and satin and filled with chocolates. She let everyone she spoke to know about the chocolates, but no one ever tasted any. Unless it was Annie.

Rachel and Annie lived together for a few years, both of them increasingly reclusive, just the aging woman and a pretty young thing, slender as a willow. At first there was a good deal of sympathy for the two women, isolated and alone. But sympathy was rapidly replaced by caution, and caution by avoidance.

There was something wrong at Aunt Annie's place.

It took a while for the rest of Shadow Valley to notice, but there was definitely something wrong.

First off, the animals died.

Not of a sudden, nothing like that. Maybe even some of them just wandered off. Probably the wolves that still haunted the lower mountains got a few that first winter.

But when Old Man Willard drove out in the spring of 1913, there wasn't any stock at all. He puttered around in the barn some, taking his sweet time collecting the odds and ends of ironwork he was buying from Rachel. When he got back to his place that night, he seemed much quieter than usual. Four years later, after he died, his wife first mentioned the dreams that plagued his final years. They had begun the night after that visit. He had never gone out to Rachel's again.

No one ever did.

Well, not quite. After Grandma married and moved back to Shadow Valley, she drove out once or twice to see Rachel. She never went beyond the house but even from there she could tell that the place was going downhill fast. Fences were falling over or were covered with thorns and brambles, the barn looked like it was ready to collapse with the next winter's snows (even though it stood until 1934, when it burned to the ground), the wagons and harrows and plows rusted, cracking, and useless.

Things like that.

And Rachel had changed, Grandma said. Grandma was well into her seventies when she finally spoke to me about all of this.

'Gone to fat, she was,' Grandma said with more than a touch of satisfaction giving her voice a saccharine whining quality so unlike her. 'Gone to fatness and softness. Big, too. Big as a house. And her always so proud of her figure. Must've been them chocolates.'

'Chocolates?' I remember asking, a boy entranced by a brief vision of a world long dead.

She studied me over the frames of her bifocals. 'Chocolates,' she repeated, her voice harsh.

I couldn't get any more from her, except that Rachel had become monstrously fat by the time the war came, 1914, the year she reached across the old wood-burner for a pot of oatmeal one morning and dragged her sleeve across the heated surface. The ancient ecru lace she always wore at the cuff flickered into flame, and before she could move an inch toward the bucket of water that was supposed to stand right next to the stove but was unaccountably clear across the kitchen on the counter next to the Hoosier cabinet, she was a screeching pillar of fire, her dress burning off her body in an instant, her flesh sizzling and popping and cracking like the strips of bacon curling in the frying pan not half a foot away.

The floor was a little scorched, but Annie was able to put the fire out with no other damage to the house.

Of course, no one was there to see what really happened. Everyone relied on what Annie could tell them through her tears and her shock. Annie repeated again and again that she had warned her mother about fire. But Rachel just wouldn't listen.

They buried what was left of Rachel three days later in the old church, the hand-cut rock one, not the brick one that went up over its blasted-out remains in 1952. Grandma said that the casket was closed, which was probably just as well, considering. But some of the folks said that even under the circumstances, it was a mighty small casket for a woman of Rachel's size.

They buried Rachel, and Annie, now a beautiful girl of seventeen, went back alone to the old house. To my knowledge, no one ever saw her again, face to face, except Grandma. For some reason that not even Grandma ever understood, she and Annie got along well. Maybe they were close enough in age, maybe Annie was envious of Grandma and her new husband and wanted to experience Grandma's life vicariously through the stories Grandma told. Whatever the reason, Grandma would drive out to the old place every once in a while, whipping the buggy team along with a practiced hand. She always went alone.

They would sit in the north parlour, what had once been Mattie's parlour, and talk about this and that, nothing special, then Annie would get a far away look in her eyes and Grandma would hitch herself up and say 'Thanks for the nice afternoon, Annie,' and leave.

Now, I got most of this from Grandma in the year or two before she died. She wasn't really that sharp any more, of course, and I wouldn't swear by all of what she said, but it's more than anyone else ever knew for sure about Aunt Annie. Until she finally opened up to me, I don't think Grandma had spoken to anyone in Shadow Valley about those drives.

Well, life went on, as it always does. Grandma had children. Some died, two lived, my mother and my Aunt Mae. Grandpa died a lonely death somewhere in the Pacific in 1944. No body was ever returned, so the marble stone in the Shadow Valley graveyard stands sentinel atop an empty casket. My mother died in childbirth. I was born in Shadow Valley, in the old house Grandpa built the first year he was married. Aunt Mae died when her only child Anna was only three days old. Grandma took the infant in.

For her last few years, Grandma seemed even closer to Annie than before. She drove out at least once a week, until she fell and broke her hip getting out of the car after one of the visits. She seemed angry as she slammed the car door and swivelled toward the icy sidewalk. Her foot skidded out from under her and she smashed down on her hip. The sound crackled through the brittle-cold air. She was almost ninety at the time. She was strong and feisty, but it took only that one slip to put her out of things for good. She died the next year.

Anna moved in with Grandpa's only surviving nephew. And that's when things started going wrong again.

All we knew of Aunt Annie at the time was that she had become as huge as her mother. Grandma wouldn't say much more, certainly not to outsiders, certainly not to the child, Anna. No one ever went out to Aunt Annie's place, except the Tuttle boy, who left a case of groceries on a wagon (or a sled, if it was winter) that was always just inside the front drive each Monday morning. No one saw Aunt Annie, even though some of us kids took it as a mark of oncoming manhood to stake-out the wagon and watch for her. But something always happened — a sudden storm, a cow bellowing for help in a field across the road, something to draw our attention from the wagon for a second, and then it would be gone. I think I almost saw her once, or her shadow, a great bloated wash of darkness moving through the trees surrounding the house.

Perhaps I only imagined it.

9

Lila closed the journal, marking the place with her forefinger. She looked around the room, more carefully this time.

This was Mattie's Parlour. The northern one with the window that looked out on brilliant sunsets during the summer — when the drapes were open. The one with the velvet-covered couch that Rachel had treasured and moved into the other woman's parlour — the other *wife's* parlour — the moment the room was hers.

This was the house the writer — whoever he or she had been — was talking about.

Lila stood, setting the journal on the cushion next to where she had been sitting. She began walking around the room, taking a closer look as she did.

There, above the fireplace, she thought she could see where a large frame had once hung. The panelling was slightly darker than elsewhere in the room, as if it had been protected from what little sunlight had been allowed to enter over the years. That would be where Rachel's portrait had been, commanding the room with her gaze.

Lila wondered what had happened to it? Had Annie discarded it? Had she actually hated — or feared — her mother so much that she couldn't stand sitting on the velvet sofa, knowing that Rachel's eyes were on her all of the time? Or had Anna gotten rid of it, having never known the living Rachel?

A slight *squeak* drew Lila's attention away from the wall.

She turned and listened intently. Thus far, she realized, that had been about the only sound she had heard in the house.

Yes, there it was again. A faint, drawn out sound, like a door swinging slightly on a rusted hinge. She concentrated all of her senses on the sound.

It was coming from upstairs.

She didn't rush out of the parlour, but neither did she delay. She moved quickly but carefully, through the open pocket doors, down the hall, and up the stairs. At the top of the stairway, she glanced along the empty hallway.

'Ella?' She didn't actually expect to hear the other woman's voice answering so she wasn't disappointed when her call was met by silence. But something *was* different about the hall.

A thin shaft of light fell onto the floor midway along its length. One of the doors was open, just enough for light within the room to escape. It was the middle room on the left. Lila remembered the sketchy description of the upstairs rooms from the journal. That would be Annie's room, the one she never used because she slept with her mother, Rachel. They would no doubt have used the door further down the hall, the one to the front-corner bedroom, which would in all probability be larger, roomier, perhaps with the luxury of two windows, one facing the front yard and the other the side.

Yet it was the middle door that stood ajar.

Lila hesitated before moving. She felt as if she were being guided . . . no,

manipulated was the better word. Someone or something wanted her to open that
middle door, to look inside the room, to
see whatever was awaiting her . . . whatever horrors might meet her eyes.

Because she was sure that whatever was
about to be revealed would be horrible.

She took a tentative step. Then two.
Then she found herself outside the
middle room, her forefinger resting lightly
on the door. She couldn't see inside, not
yet. The crack between door and frame
wasn't wide enough for her to see
anything. The narrowest strip of light
defined the entry but nothing more.

Gingerly, she pushed.

The room was . . . comfortable. Lila
wasn't certain how she would feel
actually living — or sleeping — in it, but
it looked . . . comfortable.

There was a double bed, neatly made,
with what looked to be a hand-stitched
quilt as a coverlet. It was one of the few
quilt designs whose name she could
remember: a Double Wedding-Ring, with
interlocking circles formed of small
patches of material, faded and obviously

worn but still in good repair. She recognized several bits as calico, and a couple of others that looked like plain muslin. She was sure that each piece of fabric would have its own history and its own tale if she could only speak to the woman who had stitched it.

The bed had a shallow depression in the middle, as if a single body had slept in precisely the same position night after night, year after year. And the one pillow, protected by a slightly yellowed pillow-case with an embroidered motif on one end, looked as if someone had been resting their head on it only a moment ago. Lila decided not to look any closer — she didn't want to see a single grey hair, or smell the lingering scent of long-dead roses.

On the wall opposite, where it would be seen first thing by anyone awakening in the bed, hung the portrait. Lila did not doubt that it was the one mentioned in the journal.

Rachel seemed to glower down from the wall. The picture had faded over the years, its original black and white taking on distinct tones of olive and ochre. The result was not pleasant and did little to alleviate the pointed glare in the eyes, the sharp angle of the iron-like jaw, the two narrow lines between the eyebrows that gave her a tyrannous, dictatorial look.

Lila shivered even though the air in the bedroom was temperate. She did *not* want to know anything more about Rachel. Beautiful as the woman might have been in life, her representation on the wall seemed disdainful, uncaring of the needs of others, one step short of being cruel . . . and that a mighty short step.

Lila turned away, unable to look at the woman's frozen face any longer.

In addition to the bed and the portrait, Lila saw a large wardrobe. When she opened it, she saw a row of homemade dresses hanging neatly from wooden hangers, with several drawers underneath. She was half-tempted to open the drawers but did not. That would be *too* much like snooping.

Next to the wardrobe stood an

old-fashioned sewing machine. She could read the name — *Singer* — in gilt lettering on the black enamel-like surface, surrounded with a flurry of faint golden lines forming arabesques. It was a treadle machine. She glanced around. There was no sign of an electrical outlet on the wall, although the room was lit by several sconces, so obviously the machine was intended to run on foot-power.

She remembered playing with her grandmother's machine as a child — one much like this one. She had been small enough that she would huddle on the wide treadle and rock it back and forth, imagining as she did so the needle just over her head plunging down, then pulling up to prepare for another assault on the imaginary fabric Lila pretended to be sewing.

This one moved just as easily. It made almost no sound as she pushed with her foot, the threadless needle continuing its perpetual up-and-down rhythm for a few moments after she had removed her foot. Like so many things, once set in motion, it was difficult to stop. It could continue on its own power . . . at least for a little while.

The only remaining piece of furniture was a large dresser topped by a porcelain ewer and bowl painted — most likely hand-painted — with faded yellow roses nestled in bowers of deep green leaves. There was no mirror over the dresser, nor anywhere else in the room, for that matter, the only touch that actually bothered Lila. Other than that, it looked . . . livable. Sparse and almost chaste, but livable.

When she had decided that there was nothing more to see, she retreated into the hallway, pulling the door closed behind her. She couldn't have explained why it was important that the door be closed, but she felt impelled by . . . by the silence in the house now that the small *squeak* had stopped, by some half-forgotten memory of someone explaining that closing doors helped keep dust out?

She wasn't sure, but the instant she heard the *click* of the mechanism, she knew that she had done the right thing.

She was beginning to understand the house.

Understand the house!

What madness was that?

Making her way back downstairs, she settled again into the velvet couch. She glanced over her shoulder at the place on the wall where the portrait had once hung.

One question answered, almost as soon as it was asked.

What other questions was the house willing to answer?

She picked up the journal, located the last sentence she had read, and almost voraciously began reading again.

10

From the unknown writer's journal:

The only time I actually even saw the house itself, the experience ended in tragedy.

It must have been when Grandma was still making her weekly trips to visit with Aunt Annie. I was up for the summer, staying the whole time, just Dad and me. My friend Wren and I were sleeping over at his house, about halfway down the road between Grandma's and Aunt Annie's.

It was hot and sticky that night and sleep was long in coming. We talked until late, then decided to play Huckleberry Finn and sneak out for an adventure. Even though his folks were probably fast asleep, he insisted that we climb down the arbor alongside his second-floor window.

'That's the way Huck and Tom would do it,' he explained in a mock-conspiratorial whisper, 'even if the stairs were right outside their bedroom. Anyway, it's more fun this way.'

More fun, I thought, rather grumpily it must be added, since the thin soles of my tennis shoes had just slipped on one of the horizontal braces and as a result, a rose thorn the length of Excalibur (at least that is what it felt like) had jammed itself to the bone. I was certain that I would bleed to death before we got to the bottom.

(Okay, perhaps I was a bit of a wuss back then, but remember that I was a city boy and all of this was new to me. What was simple adventure for Wren reeked of mortal peril for me.)

The thin wooden slats creaked and grumbled with our weight, threatening at any instant to break and throw us the remaining few feet to the ground, but eventually our feet touched solid if soggy earth. I don't think either of us had any clear ideas at that moment about where to go, what to do. We just started walking down the moon-drenched road, talking aimlessly in muted whispers, elbowing each other occasionally and laughing as if we had just pulled the world's greatest practical joke on each other, randomly kicking pebbles with the sides of our sneakers.

'Sure is hot,' I said, wiping sweat from my brow even though it had to have been almost midnight. July can do that in Shadow Valley, where the nights could be as hot and muggy as the days.

'Hey,' Wren said all of a sudden. 'I know! Let's go swimming.'

I wasn't sure about the whole idea. It was late and in spite of the bright moonlight, the shadows lurking under the trees seemed impenetrably dark. I think I was imagining the municipal pool back home, all white and blue tile with black lines painted on the bottom to keep the swimmers from crashing into each other. But even there, in my imagination at least, the lights would be off at midnight, and the pool water would be dark. Out here, wherever Wren was leading us, the water would be an unfathomable mystery, with a bottomless blackness that would reflect the night sky. I was enough of a city boy that I wasn't quite sure about a lot of things Wren took for granted, but I couldn't let on to Wren. He and I had palled around every summer since his folks moved to Shadow Valley seven years before, and even though we saw each other only a month or two in a year, he was probably my closest friend.

I wonder now if he ever knew just how important he was to me. And I wish that he could have been there when my world exploded and I was suddenly alone.

'Well . . . okay.' It was not a whole-hearted, total commitment, but I figured it would be enough to get me by.

'There's this great place, just over the rise,' he said. We walked a bit further. Off in the distance behind us, bullfrogs croaked along the edges of one of the irrigation ditches that crisscrossed the valley. Closer by, an animal bellowed. I jumped.

'Just a calf, stupid,' Wren said, hitting the last word just enough to let me know it was a joke. I punched him in the shoulder. He punched me back.

The air was growing cooler, not chilly

by any means, just not so breath-stealing hot. And I could feel moisture in the slight breeze as well. Mosquitoes buzzed near our ears but none settled. We kept going.

Abruptly, Wren cut away from the road we had been following and ducked down a narrow path through a stand of box elders that seemed skeletal and ghostly in the filtered light. He stopped at the crest of a low rise. I pulled up next to him.

I think I saw the house first. Its black shingled roof seemed like an abyss swallowing any stray moonlight. Its visible windows were black. They looked as if they had never allowed a single shard of light in or out. Its broken chimneys thrust up like decaying teeth against the cloudless sky.

I swallowed, hard.

'Uh . . . that's . . . that's . . . Isn't that Aunt Annie's place?' I said. I'd never actually *been* there, but I'd heard enough about it from Grandma, mostly by listening in the other room after one of her visits, when she talked to Dad about where she had been and what she had seen. I had never seen the place, and I never *wanted* to see it.

Yet there it stood, in its darkened hollow, teeth bared to receive unwelcome visitors.

'Yeah,' Wren finally said. He was trying to sound nonchalant but his voice cracked at the last moment, breaking the illusion. Then his voice shifted. I could almost see him straightening his shoulders and becoming, in his own mind at least, the tough guy that we both dreamed of someday being. 'Yeah, it's her place. So what?'

Now you've got to remember that Wren was my friend, that his family had only lived in the valley for a few years, buying one of the old pioneer places and somehow turning it into a paying farm. I knew him, and I knew them, and I loved them and trusted them.

But they weren't family.

I should have said something. God knows I wish to this day that I had. I should have pleaded illness, cowardice, a suddenly and miraculously broken leg . . . anything to keep from taking another step toward that house, but I didn't. As distant as the connection might be, Aunt Annie was Family.

'Well . . . ' I began, weakly enough.

'Come on, don't chicken out. It's not like it's *haunted* or anything. We don't even have to get that close to it. The pond's way out behind the shed. You can see it from the top of the hill. The water should still be pretty deep this time of year. It'll be great. No one will ever know that we were here.'

How wrong he was.

He took off like a startled deer, jumping ahead so fast that I almost didn't see which direction he had gone. Still only half willing, I followed.

We skirted the house, all right, only getting close enough to see that the windows were as dark and silent and non-reflecting as if they had been draped in death-crepe. There wasn't a suggestion of light anywhere. Even the moon seemed to darken when we stepped out from the protective shadows of the box elders and stood for a moment in the open space between the house and the shed next to the barren spot where the barn had burned long years before. Then we ducked across what once might have been a lawn and disappeared into shadows again.

I think Wren must have felt something, because as soon as we were hidden from view of the house behind half a dozen man-sized trunks, he said, 'Hey, you know, let's . . . '

Then he broke off and looked at me. He might have seen the relief that flooded through me at his words, because he seemed to change his mind. His voice took on a new tone and he squared his thin shoulders again. 'Let's go on. Last one in's a rotten egg.'

He ran toward the black, swelling shadow that was the shed and disappeared around the side. I followed more slowly. I couldn't keep from glancing over my shoulder at the dark windows as they became visible between the trees, watching for a flicker of drapery, a hint of match held against the hand-twisted wick of an old-fashioned tallow candle.

I watched, and slowly followed Wren.

And then, before I even got around the corner of the shed, I heard a sound like a stifled whimper. It was soft, low, agonized, almost inaudible but it seemed to echo and re-echo like a drawn-out death-scream in the absolute silence of the night.

I froze. I wanted to make my legs go on, make them skirt the side of the shed and bear me to whatever had made that sound, but they wouldn't listen to me.

I couldn't move.

A second sound shattered my stasis, louder this time, more ponderous and infinitely more threatening.

'Wren!' I screamed, 'Wren!' and without thinking I careened around the shed.

Wren was at the edge of the pond, naked. His clothing lay scattered in a ragged line from the edge of the shed to the edge of the pond. It looked as if he had toed out of his sneakers (neither of us wore socks that night), then pulled off pants and T-shirt and underpants on the run and, without pausing to think about how dangerous it might be, dived long and flat into the still black midnight waters of the pond.

Even from a distance, the light was bright enough for me to see that his head was crushed.

He must have struck a rock, then somehow found enough life to crawl out onto the bank and die.

I stood there, staring, numb, watching the moonlight glisten on his blood as it pooled beneath his head and shoulders and sank into the dark, waiting soil.

Only later, much later, after I had fallen to my knees and vomited until I felt my guts rip loose; only after I ran home to Grandma's and woke Dad and Grandma with my wild shrieks and heaving, gasping breaths that threatened to become uncontrollable spasms; only after Dad raced out, dressed only in his underpants, and drove like a madman down the road while I waited in the kitchen with Grandma, my body trembling and threatening to let go of its tenuous grasp on consciousness; only when Dad returned far more slowly and walked into the kitchen and dropped heavily into the chair and took the phone from its cradle on the wall and slowly dialed Wren's folk's number . . . only after all of that did I remember three things.

First, even though the night was so silent that I could hear the *swish swish swish* of my sneakered feet in the stubbly grass, I hadn't heard Wren dive into the water.

Second, his back and legs were dry when I saw him. The moon had reflected wetly from the blood pulsing from the hideous wound on his head, but not from white skin as dry and pale as ancient parchment.

And third, I had seen something. A huge shadow that disappeared beneath the trees the instant I came around the side of the shed.

That last memory was tenuous, fragmented, and I no sooner touched it than I shoved it away with all of my might.

There couldn't have been anything.

I must have imagined it in the instant of shock.

No one saw Aunt Annie for the whole time between Dad arriving at the pond and Wren's burial in the graveyard halfway up the hill on the other side of the valley; or, for years afterward, anyone but Grandma. She didn't come out of her house when the county sheriff pulled up in his patrol car and looked at the pond. She didn't answer when he knocked at the door to ask if she had seen or heard anything the night Wren died. She spoke to him later on the telephone from Grandma's kitchen, two hushed minutes of him asking questions, her apparently answering with a curt, whispered 'yes' or 'no,' then him hanging up the phone with an odd look of frustration on his face.

But there never seemed to be any real question that Wren's death was more than a horrible accident. From the bank, in the bright light of day, the sheriff could even see the outline of the rock that must have killed Wren.

So my best friend was buried. Aunt Annie did not attend the funeral. No one expected her to. But when Grandma came back from visiting Annie later the next week, she shooed me outside angrily and wouldn't speak a word to Dad or me until after dinner that night, a dinner that had to have been the worst she ever cooked in her life. The roast was burned, the mashed potatoes thin and sour, the gravy heavy and clotted with lumps of flour. Even then, hours after her return from Aunt Annie's, I saw spots of high color in Grandma's cheeks and flecks of what might have been anger . . . or a deep, abiding fear in her eyes.

But that's the past. Wren is only a memory.

A bitter, biting memory.

11

This time, something startled Lila, jerking her consciousness from the journal to the reality of the night-shadowed room around her. It was a sound. Definitely a sound. Something like a moan.

'Ella!' Lila was standing in an instant, the journal dropping helter-skelter to the floor. 'Ella, cut that out! If you are trying to scare me for some reason, you're going to have to do a *damn* better job of it than this!

'Come out from wherever it is you're hiding. Now!'

She waited, listening, but heard no tell-tale scuffing of shoes on wooden planks, no shuffle across thread-worn carpets.

'I mean it, Ella!' except that this time, there was less anger in her voice and more fear — terrible, quavering fear that began somewhere near her heart and radiated outward into her bones and sinews.

'Ella?'

From somewhere overhead, the sound repeated. This time she heard it, not clearly perhaps, but enough to tell that it was organic, *human*, the sound breath makes when it passes through lungs and throat already agonized by pain.

'Is that you, Ella? Is something wrong? Please!'

Reflexively, Lila reached into her pocket for her cell phone, already forgetting how useless that appendage of technology had proven earlier. She glanced down to make sure the cell was charged and showing bars. Three bars. She punched redial again, wishing with all her heart that there was someone out there who would be trying to contact *her*, who would realize that she should have returned from Shadow Valley hours ago and who would raise heaven and earth to find her.

But, she knew, there was no one. She and her mother spoke by telephone, infrequently and more than occasionally rancorously. Her father was long gone; so was her grandmother. No one at work knew much about her after hours, a situation she had conscientiously cultivated.

There had been Geoff, of course, but that interlude had been over months ago . . . about the time she had become so involved in the plans for Shadow Valley.

Other than that, no one knew her. No one cared.

The cell rang once. Twice. Then . . . static.

She almost threw the phone across the room, then caught herself just in time. She was slipping it back into her pocket even as she half ran from the parlour and began climbing the stairs.

Halfway up she stopped to listen. She could hear the hammering of her heart, the pounding of blood in the vessels near her ears. But nothing else. Whatever had been moaning was silent now.

She continued up the stairs. At the top, she stepped immediately to the window, because now it was no longer a blank, black screen. Instead, something outside glowed faintly, just enough so that, with her back to the hall light, she could detect it.

She leaned close to the pane. The sill was dusty, far dustier than anything else she had seen in the house, and she refused to touch it with her fingers. There were dead things in the dust as well . . . large roaches that looked so alive that she half expected them to leap at her; bluebottle flies battered by their doomed struggle with the impervious glass; even a honey bee that had found its way into the house somehow and did not survive the encounter.

She stared outside, trying to figure out where the glow was coming from. Something white, unmoving, a distance away. Nearer, she saw a dark, hulking silhouette that had to have been one of the outbuildings . . . probably a shed of some sort. A little distance further, the skeletal outlines of trees, thick-trunked and looking eerie in the darkness. Beyond that, a glimmer of something that was probably water.

A pond . . .

The pond . . .

The pond where the boy — what was his name? it was a bird of some sort, a songbird — *Wren*, yes that was it. Where *Wren* was found dead. So that meant that the motionless white object, the long, thin thing stretched on the ground just this side of the pond had to be . . .

She screamed and pulled back from the window, her hand covering her mouth to keep the vast bulk of the scream from escaping and shattering the window.

The boy's body.

But that was impossible. *Impossible.* The journal was probably years old, and the tale it told even older than that. The boy was long since buried, a small, pitiable pile of dry and dusty bones in a coffin slowly melding itself with the earth around it.

The boy could *not* be there, could not be resting, dead, by the pond.

She turned . . . and almost screamed again.

Three thin shafts of light fell on the hallway floor, one from each of the previously sealed doors on the north side of the house. The farthest one would be the room directly above the parl . . . *Mattie's Parlour.*

Whatever was in that room, whoever had turned on the light and opened the door just the tiniest of cracks had been standing right over her head as she read.

She straightened — if one little boy could talk himself into acting like a 'tough guy,' then she certainly could.

She approached the first shaft of light, the one closest to the stairs.

At the door, she paused, took a deep breath, and reminded herself that the other time she had opened an unlocked door, nothing had happened. The room revealed as she pushed back the panel had been nothing more frightening than a rather old-style, somewhat staid and somber bedchamber, complete with antique wardrobe and treadle sewing machine. Besides, she reassured herself, the journal had mentioned that the three bedrooms along the northern side of the house had originally been for Mattie and her children, and they had all moved away decades ago.

More likely than not, the three rooms

would be empty, or failing that would exhibit all of the graceless charm of guest rooms that had never actually seen a guest.

She could deal with this. She was ready.

She pushed lightly on the center panel of the heavy door. It swung silently open.

Lila was screaming and crying and pounding on the front door before she became aware that she had even moved, that she had bolted down the stairs at literally break-neck speed and run the length of the downstairs hallway, only to discover that the front door — so amenable to her desires all day long — had suddenly turned rebellious, recalcitrant. Her fingers scrabbled frantically with the lock but it would not turn *it would not turn!*

She was locked inside a madhouse with that . . . that abomination . . . that horror upstairs.

Surely she would go mad . . . or was already mad.

Then reason reasserted itself.

Wait. She forced herself to think. She

had seen something out the window, some trick of the light on a boulder, some reflection of the moon on a curiously shaped patch of grass, and her imagination had formed from that the supine body of a boy dead — *accidentally dead* — years, decades before. Then, some perverse trick of shadow had convinced her that she had opened a door and seen . . .

Nonsense. She was made of stronger stuff than that.

She willed herself to cross the hallway and ascend the stairs. At the top, she noticed that whatever oddity of angle had caused the glow to reflect through the window was gone. The filthy pane was black and unreflecting again, just as it had been earlier in the day.

She took three steps and stood before the open door.

This time she did not scream. To scream was beyond her powers. She could only stand and stare and pray that what she was seeing *was* the illusion she had tried to convince herself that it must be.

The bed was wet, sodden, with a

mixture of greenish slime-clotted water and scarlet blood. The carpet was wet as well, and she could see clearly a set of footprints — man-sized and wearing boots — on the hardwood planks just inside the door. They stopped at the threshold, as if whoever had stepped there had simply appeared at that juncture in the universe, uncreated and unwanted. There were no return prints.

But that was not the worst thing.

Oh, no. That was barely the beginning.

In the middle of the bed, its head cushioned on a soft pillow of the lightest, most delicate blue, its arms stretched out to either side, lay the body of a boy. He was eight, perhaps, or ten, or twelve. It was almost impossible to tell since his naked flesh was hollowed and gouged with wrinkles deeper than any Lila had ever thought possible. His eyelids were open, revealing flat white eyes with no irises and only the smallest fleck of darkness for pupils. His palms and feet were the white of subterranean fish.

And his head . . . *his poor little head* . . . was oozing blood that dribbled down his cheek to mix with the filthy mess in which he was lying.

Finally Lila moved. She grasped the edge of the door and yanked it toward herself, barely removing her fingers in time to avoid them being bruised, possibly crushed, by the massive wood. The door swung shut. She heard the click of the lock and knew that if she tried to open it again — *although why she would want to do so, God only knew* — it would be as immoveable as before.

She folded her arms tightly across her chest and clutched her elbows convulsively, as if the tighter she could grasp herself the surer she could be of her existence, her life.

She nearly fainted.

She might have, except at that moment a second sound, louder and more compelling, emerged from the middle bedroom.

'Lila.'

Or possibly it might have been 'Ella.'

The sound — the voice — was muffled, as if the speaker's mouth were shrouded with cloth or stuffed with cotton, the way morticians one time did to ensure that cadavers would bear some passing resemblance to the images mourners carried in their minds of the deceased.

Lila froze on the spot.

The sound came again. And even though she was straining to listen, she could not distinguish between the words: 'Lila . . . Ella . . . Lila . . . la . . . la . . . la'

This time, it seemed as if there were two voices, speaking almost in tandem but not quite, the sounds off just enough that there was a slight stutter.

'El-Li-la-la.'

She couldn't help herself. She moved slowly toward the middle door, toward the splinter of light that spilled onto the hall and guided her steps. As she drew near, the sound — the voices — whatever it had been . . . stopped. Silence.

She touched the door, pushed lightly.

It swung full open, revealing the horrors within.

This time she was marginally prepared. She neither screamed nor nearly fainted. She did, however, shut her eyes and half avert her head for a moment, giving herself time to prepare.

Again the focus of the room was the double bed set squarely in the centre. On either side were hand-made circular rugs braided of colourful remnants coiling around and around hypnotically, drawing the eye inexorably toward the centre, toward a tight clot of darkness that was the first twisted knot. In another time and another place, they might have been positioned to protect the sleepers' feet from the icy chill of bare boards on a winter morning — but neither sleeper in this room would ever feel heat or cold again.

Two young men, one barely out of his teens, the other some years younger, lay side by side on a quilted coverlet. This time, the quilt, the bed, the floor were dry, unstained by blood or by the polluted, noxious black water of a moonlit tarn. The figures lay nearly touching, naked, their flesh silvery white in the light of a single sconce near the door. They seemed almost identical, sharing the same high cheekbones, the same thin nose, the same smoothly muscled arms and chests and thighs. But there the resemblance ended.

The figure — the younger boy — on the left had clearly died in agony. His eyes bulged from the sockets, pupils fixed and staring. His head was canted back at an obviously painful angle to accommodate the hideous swelling around his throat. The flesh looked taut, tight, as if a single touch would be sufficient for it to burst and spill its accumulation of blood and ichor and corruption onto the coverlet. On one leg, an ulcer the size of Lila's fist had eaten into the flesh of the calf, its center a core of granular tissue, red and suppurating.

Diphtheria.

Lila had never seen anyone who had died of the disease, had never known anyone who had died of it. She was born long after vaccinations and treatments had all but eradicated the disease, at least in the United States. She wasn't sure she had ever even heard anyone talk about it. But she knew what she was seeing.

Who she was seeing.

Edmond. Mattie's youngest son. Dead

a month after his father. Dead a week after he had gone innocently fishing with his closest friend, perhaps stealing a few light-hearted moments for some skinny-dipping in some willow-sheltered hollow of one of the nearby creeks, perhaps diving with boyish unconcern into the same pool that would be the site of young Wren's death decades later.

Edmond, dead of diphtheria.

Lila felt as if she need not even look at the boy's companion in death. She knew who she would see. And what. But she couldn't stop herself. Whatever compulsion had brought her to the doorway forced her to shift her gaze to the right. As she did so, she took a step closer, crossing over the threshold and entering the room.

The second figure — the older boy, the young man — had to be Albert. Enough remained of his face for her to see clearly that he was the boy's brother, but much of the flesh around the jaw and throat was ragged and torn, as if ripped from the body by fangs and claws . . . coyotes, perhaps, scavenging a meal from the bloody corpse. Hands, feet, the soft tissue of the abdomen — all had been savaged by the same fangs and claws long before the body had been discovered and returned home.

As Lila had known it would be, the right leg twisted awkwardly, as if the remaining muscle were incapable of holding ankle and foot in their proper positions. The single fatal gash was no longer bleeding — had bled out nearly a century before — and the severed flesh had a peculiar sheen that made it seem as if it were illumined from deep within. As she watched, she could almost see the toes twitch reflexively, convulsively, reacting even in death to the shock of the axe-blade that had cut the young man's life short.

Albert, dead at his own hand.

And Rachel had warned him.

Rachel had warned them *both*.

Lila shivered. She shut her eyes and counted to ten — her panacea for all moments of panic — then opened them, hoping that the room, the bed, the silent bodies of the young men would disappear.

They did not.

Albert and Edmond lay silently, motionlessly. Abruptly, in a way that she had not felt for the hideously deformed body of young Wren, Lila felt ashamed for gazing upon them in their nakedness. They should be covered, protected, hidden from all prying eyes.

She almost took another step into the room, intending to look for another quilt that she could lay like a shroud over the two boys, before she came to her senses.

They were *dead*. They had been dead for twice — perhaps even three times — as long as she had been alive. They felt no shame. Nor should she. Present or not, illusion or reality, hallucination or some construct of a house haunted by its own past and its own history . . . whatever they were, she had nothing to do with them, shared no connections with them beyond the bond of common humanity. She could turn around, close the door, and leave them, whether it be in the light of that single bulb dissipating the shadows that crowded the corners of the room, or in the absolute darkness and

141

emptiness that she was half convinced would prevail once the door had shut.

So she did. She turned her back on the bed and its grotesque occupants and, without the slightest hint of a glance over her shoulder, exited the room, pulling the door shut behind her. She did, however, listen for the nearly inaudible *snick* that told her that if she were to try to open the door again, it would be as obdurate as all of the others in the house had been.

That left one room.

She didn't want to go there. She knew that she was being manipulated by . . . something. She knew that whatever was happening in the house was beyond anything that she could understand or explain. She even knew what — *who* — she would see in the room that had once been shared by Mattie and . . .

She suddenly realized that she had no idea of the name of the man who had apparently set all of this, whatever it was, in motion. The journal never mentioned his name. He was simply 'Great-granddad', the patriarch who, not satisfied with Mattie's love and companionship, had sought out another wife . . . and another. And who had then brought Rachel into his house, the woman without a past, without a history (so far as the journal-writer knew, who was himself an unknown), without a family. The woman who had presided over the systematic destruction of everyone and everything that stood in the way of her wishes for herself and for her daughter. Aunt Annie.

Lila knew almost nothing about the man. But she was certain of what she would see in the front corner bedroom, directly above the parlor in which she had been reading the sordid story of this family.

She approached the door. There was the familiar slit of light. The familiar fragmentary glimpse into a room that by all rights should be empty of all but the ghosts of dreams and the phantasms of lost hopes.

Strangely, she felt no fear. If anything, she was curious. And angry. And determined.

Whoever or whatever was putting her through this obstacle course of locked-door/open-door didn't know her, didn't

understand her at all. Natural or super-
natural, she would face what she had to
face and emerge *herself*. Regardless.

She opened the door, placing the flat of
her palm against a center panel and
pushing so hard that the door rebounded
from the inner wall.

12

She had been right.

Oh, she had missed on a few of the details, of course. But that was to be expected.

Instead of a plain double bed with an equally plain headboard made of hand-hewn pine, as she had seen in the other two rooms, this bed clearly belonged to the lord and master of the realm. The headboard was tall, nearly six feet tall, constructed of dark, richly grained oak meticulously detailed with carved leaves and flowers and arabesques and curlicues. It had to have been purchased back east, sometime during the last decades of the nineteenth century, and shipped out to the wild-and-wooly west, either by train or, just possibly, by wagon. In spite of a thin layer of dust on its curved lines, it was polished underneath, well-cared for. The kind of bed appropriate for the master to share with his wife . . . his *first* wife. In the eyes of the law, his *only* wife.

And one that Rachel would have coveted intensely, even if hers had been nearly identical. It still would not have been *this* bed.

Instead of a hand-stitched quilt, this one was covered by a crocheted bedspread in a complex design that complemented the ornate carving on the headboard. Possibly Mattie had made it herself, meticulously crafting each of the tiny medallions, then stitching them together until they covered the bed and hung over on both sides, nearly touching the floor. She might have brought it as part of her dowry, when she had come to . . . whatever his name was, as a young bride. They might have lain beneath it as they consummated their marriage, as they joined again and again in creating new life.

Including the two man-boys — or simulacra thereof — Lila had just seen.

She entered the room and stood less than an arm's length from the side of the bed.

As had been the others, the man — Great-granddad, for lack of a better name — was naked. He had been verging on old age when he had died. His long hair and full beard had once been white, Lila was sure, but in this incarnation they were yellowed and sickly looking, like attenuated, interwoven vines that had germinated beneath some huge boulder and that had struggled to attain mature growth having never seen the sun. In spite of his obvious age, he was still well-muscled, obviously someone who had worked, and worked hard, every day of his adult life.

She imagined that anyone else looking upon the corpse would have commented on how life-like he appeared . . . as long as they could not see the hideous gash that nearly split him in half. Beginning at just below his throat and continuing like some widening canyon eroded by æons of winds and water, it split his ribcage, cutting deeply into the muscles of his heart and exposing his lungs on both sides. His intestines were sliced into fragments. His genitalia were little more than mangled masses of unidentifiable flesh, nameable only by location and not by shape or form.

The plow.

It had destroyed him — *riven him* — as thoroughly as it must have destroyed myriads of terrified rodents huddling in their silent burrows as it tore through the fallow earth each spring in preparation for sowing.

Lila looked down at his face, trying to ignore the ghastly ruin that was his torso. He did not look evil. Or even particularly bad. He merely looked like a man of his times, driven by passion or by faith or by who-knew-what other powerful emotion to contravene the *mores* of his day. He could not have known what — according to the anonymous journal — his appetites would lead to. He could not have imagined the generations of death and destruction and despair that would follow the simple act of bringing Rachel into . . .

The hand closest to Lila moved.

She watched in horror as it lifted itself from the crocheted coverlet, its knuckles swollen and arthritic-looking, its fingers long and strong and blunt from working the soil in an age before machines stole the privilege of hard labour from men. Tendons in the forearm stood out against chalk-white skin. Biceps bulged with the effort.

As paralyzed as a mouse watching the approach of the serpent that intended its death, she watched the hand move, slowly at first, then more rapidly, reaching across the expanse of the bed toward . . .

. . . *her*.

She broke her paralysis at the last possible moment, just as the fingers curved to nestle themselves around her wrist and . . . and *what?* — and pull her down onto the deathbed in an unbreakable embrace that would pinion her and suffocate her and . . . ?

She moved just as everything around her began to turn black.

In her next moment of conscious awareness, she was standing in the middle of the hallway, shaking as if every molecule of her self were exerting its last degree of strength to throw off the touch — even the *imagined touch* — of the thing lying on the bed.

The door to the front corner room was closed. She had no memory of pulling it to or of hearing the by-now familiar *snick* of the bolt, but it was nonetheless securely shut. The thin cracks on both sides, on top and bottom, nearly invisible against the dark wood of the door itself, told her that the room was now sealed. She would not be able to enter, even if she wished to.

Which she — most profoundly — did *not* wish to do.

As shaken as she was, she still found the presence of mind to walk, not run, to the stairway and cautiously descend. Her legs shook with each step downward, as if she had just finished running a marathon. Her cheeks felt fiery and flushed. Her breast heaved with the effort of drawing air into her lungs. For the first time, she became aware that the inside of the house was musty, oppressive, heavy with a sense of disuse and abandonment.

Without thinking, she walked to the front door, calmly twisted the lock, and stepped outside onto the porch.

Only when she took her first deep,

cleansing breath of the night air did it register.

The door had opened for her this time.

Did that mean that the house was ready to let her go?

She glanced around.

The grounds surrounding the house were solid black, as solid as if the air were painted concrete. She could see none of the trees that she knew were there, none of the stands of weeds and brush that dotted the yard. She could not see her car, although it had to be standing where she had parked it so long ago.

How long?

She pulled her cell from her pocket. It showed three power-bars but she didn't even try to call out. Instead she checked the time display.

Twelve-o'clock. And zero seconds.

The witching hour.

She knew that that couldn't actually be the correct time. Not that it might not be midnight, or even much later. But rather than it seemed impossible that she should check the time at that precise instant.

She closed her eyes and counted to ten.

Then looked at her cell again.

Twelve-o'clock. And zero seconds.

All right, then, she had no idea *what* time it might be. Anytime from sunset to sunrise. Or perhaps no time at all. Perhaps she was caught in some phantasmagorical pocket of un-Time, where past and present collided without warning and without consequence.

Another deep breath. The air was cool, tinged with moisture. Pleasant, almost. At any other time, she might have enjoyed sitting on the old swing and rocking back and forth, watching the breeze ripple through the trees.

If she could have seen the trees.

Instead, she took a third cleansing breath — recognizing the moment for what it was, an interim, a short break to allow her a modicum of restoration before . . .

Before the horrors resumed.

She turned and re-entered the house. She neither closed the door nor, when it swung silently shut behind her, bothered either to check to see if it was unlocked or to lock it. She didn't care anymore.

The house would do what it wanted.

She stopped for a moment in the main hall, waiting for some indication of what she was supposed to do next. The light in the upstairs hallway was dark. So then, what ever was next on the bill of entertainment for the evening would take place down stairs. The pocket doors to the southern room — the one she had not yet entered — looked as invincibly locked as they had before. The only possible thing she could do was to return to the . . . to Mattie's parlor and see what awaited her.

It didn't take long.

She stepped through the doorway, looked up, and saw it.

Hanging above the fireplace, in what was apparently its wonted position, was the portrait of Rachel.

13

Lila strode across the room and stationed herself in front of the fireplace immediately beneath the lithograph, staring up at it. Challenging it. Daring it to do its worst.

After all, if it could transport itself from room to room, no doubt floating ethereally, if not invisibly, from floor to floor, from room to room, what else might the monstrosity be able to do?

'Well, Rachel' — *you unspeakable bitch!* — 'What now?'

She wasn't sure what to expect, if anything, so the sullen silence that stretched throughout the house wasn't a shock. There were no inarticulate moans, no stuttering echoic versions of her name, no *clicks* or *snicks* of locks opening or closing. All she could hear was her own breathing, lessening now that she confronted the darkness outside and returned to the house of her own volition.

'Come on, woman! I haven't got all day. Or all night. Whichever it is.'

Hello, Lila.

'All right. That's better. I think it's about time that you came clean with me. I've played your nasty little games' — the overhead chandelier dimmed, then brightened again — 'yes, you heard me, *nasty little games*. I am not impressed.

'Oh, I'll admit that you had me going for a while, that you probably still have me going. But now you're going to have to do a bit more if you want me to keep playing.

'For one thing, *no more nasties!*'

She waited for a signal, a thump, a bang, a window exploding as if a bullet had shattered it, something to suggest the house's willingness or unwillingness to accept her ultimatum.

When nothing occurred, she continued.

'And for another, *where is Ella?*'

Ella — Lila — la — la — la. It sounded like an echo, beginning upstairs and filtering its way downstairs and permeating the parlor. *La — la — la.*

'That's not good enough,' Lila said.

She crossed her arms and canted her hips, throwing most of her weight onto one leg. It was, she thought, her most forceful posture. Here I am, it seemed to say, try to move me if you can. I'm here, and I'm here to stay.

She decided on another tack.

'Why did you set up that horror-show upstairs? What did you expect from me? That I would faint? Scream and run? Take off into the underbrush and run in a panic until I either died of a heart attack or fell into an abandoned well, or until someone picked me up in a day or two and carted me off to a rubber-room in the booby-hatch? What was the point of all of that?'

To let you know.

'Well, you certainly did that. You let me know that you want your way and intend to have it, regardless of whom you have to hurt. Not a particularly pretty lesson to learn, though. It doesn't reflect well upon you or your character.'

The portrait seemed to sneer, the face growing colder and even more distant than the vagaries of nineteenth-century lithography could account for.

'Now let me tell you a little bit about myself. I know what I want, too, and it has nothing to do with you. I've made my way through the world pretty much on my own, and I've done a damn good job of it. I owe no one anything. I don't have to lean on anyone to get things done. I choose my direction in life and I follow it unerringly.

'So all the little arrangements you've made to reduce me to a terrified ruin of a woman won't work. *Do you hear that, Rachel? They won't work.*'

The portrait did not respond.

Of course, it didn't answer, Lila suddenly thought. *It's only a picture!* She abruptly felt foolish for carrying on an imaginary conversation — for having an imaginary confrontation — with a woman long years dead. The portrait was no more alive and capable of responding than were those . . . those *things* upstairs.

And yet the hand moved, the fingers curled to grasp your wrist.

Her shoulders stiff with resolution, Lila turned her back on the portrait and

157

retraced her steps to the sofa.

The journal lay on the cushion next to where she had been sitting. It was open to the last page she had read.

And yet she was certain that when she had run from the room a few minutes — hours — centuries — before, it had been laying on the carpet in a heap.

She had never picked it up.

She did so now.

And she began to read again.

14

From the unknown writer's journal:

When Grandma died, Anna moved in with Grandpa's only surviving nephew and his family. She was about eleven at the time.

Seven years passed.

I visited only rarely and then alone. Dad refused to return to the valley after one last trip for Grandma's funeral. He would never explain why. Three years later, he died.

That left just Anna and me. All that remained of Grandma's family . . . and except for Annie, all that anyone seemed to know about of Great-granddad's once-extensive family.

For most of that time, Anna's life passed uneventfully.

She suffered through several schoolgirl crushes, apparently not particularly serious. And I think she probably broke a heart or two along the way. I know that she broke an arm falling out of the elm tree behind the house she was living in.

Then last fall, the dreams began.

She could not exactly remember what they had been about, she would explain when Uncle Evan or Aunt Vera would rush to her side and waken her from the dreams that left her screaming, sweating, and panting as raggedly as if she had just run a mile. 'I don't know, I don't know,' she would repeat over and over, until Vera wanted to shake her out of sheer frustration.

Night after night, the dreams came and Anna would scream and Evan and Vera would rush to her side.

After a while only Evan came. Vera lost patience with her.

As the nights passed, Anna became listless, not quite sick but certainly not well. She lost weight.

It's hard to believe that now.

Anyway, one night in mid-January, she screamed her way out of the dream again, but this time was different.

'She's dead! She's dead!'

When Evan tried to calm her, she grew even more hysterical. She wept violently and yanked at her hair with fingers as stiff as twigs from a long-dead tree, clawing at it as if there were something caught in it. Evan tried to pull her hands down and was appalled at the strength in the young girl's arms. It was like engaging in a tug-of-war with a granite monolith. He was afraid that if he tried any harder, he might injure her . . . or she might hurt him.

Finally, though, she dropped her hands and began to wring them as if she were in the final throes of desperation. After a few minutes more, she was able to talk.

'She's dead, Uncle Evan,' she said through harsh gasps. 'She's dead.'

'Who, honey? Who?'

'Aunt Annie.'

'What?'

'She's dead. I know it. We've got to get out there. Now.'

She was out of bed before Evan had a chance to argue. He grabbed at her arm and tried to draw her back, to make her lie down again, but she wrenched herself from his grip, threw a heavy robe over her shoulders, and headed for the door.

'I'm going, Uncle Evan.'

'But Anna, sweetheart, it's . . . '

'I'm going. I *have* to go. I'll walk if I have to, but I'm going. *Now!*'

Vera was standing in the hall just outside Anna's bedroom door. She held up one hand and started to say something.

'Now, Anna, you had better listen to . . . '

Anna swept past her as if the woman did not exist. Vera stared at Anna then transferred her stare to Evan as he rushed out of the girl's room. His sparse grey hair was still awry from sleep, his face haggard, his feet bare and already bluish from the cold.

'What's going on? What . . . ?'

'Come on. We've got to help her.'

'Help her do what?'

'I don't know, but she's convinced Aunt Annie's dead and she's going out to her place. Right now. We've got to stop her before she heads out on foot.'

'I don't . . . '

'No time. Get your things,' Evan said as he grabbed his wife's arm and propelled her to the kitchen.

Anna was already bundled up in boots, a heavy knee-length coat, a muffler, and a hat. Her hand was on the doorknob.

'Wait, Anna,' Evan said. 'We're coming too.'

Anna turned to glare at him. For an instant, he didn't recognize her, didn't see anything in her eyes or in the set of her jaw that even resembled the girl he and Vera had known for all those years and had grown to love as their own. He saw only a roiling, whirling darkness that terrified him more than anything he had ever encountered. He stepped back, almost left the kitchen.

Then something indefinable shifted in Anna's countenance and she was herself. Softer. Vulnerable.

'Please, Uncle Evan, please. I truly have to be there. As soon as possible. I can't tell you how important it is.'

'How important *what* is?'

'I . . . I don't know. I only know that I have to go.'

'All right,' Evan said, already pulling on his own coat. Anna waited by the door, seemingly calm, but her hand never left the door knob.

'We have to,' Evan said to Vera.

Vera looked at him questioningly, but he said no more.

Ten minutes later they were barreling down the snow-dusted road at midnight in Evan's old Chevy, their breath frosting in the icy chill. It had to be ten degrees below zero. Evan could not remember it being so cold, not for years and years at least. And he was still half numb from being awakened abruptly. Vera was stonily silent. He would have to figure out what to say to her . . . but later, perhaps in the morning. Right now all he understood was that it was imperative that he rush Anna to Aunt Annie's.

Behind them, huddled tightly in a corner of the back seat like a terrified child, Anna began whimpering.

Evan took the turnoff to Aunt Annie's so fast that the snow tires lost traction and the car skewed sideways, its front fender grazing the exposed canes of the wild-rose hedge. Stiff thorns as long as knife blades scratched at the side of the car and chattered along the window as the car sped by.

'Evan!' Vera screamed and clutched at his arm. His elbow jerked out almost without his knowledge and knocked her hand up.

'Don't,' he said. 'Don't distract me. Or we'll crash for sure.'

Vera let out a muted cry and pulled away from him, pressing herself against the passenger door as if to put as much distance as possible from this stranger who used to be her husband and from the wicked-looking thorns still grating against the car.

Through it all, Anna didn't seem to notice. Her whimpering was deeper now, a prolonged, agonizing groan so profound that if Vera and Evan hadn't been so intent on what was happening to the car, they would have felt their blood chill at the sound.

Even when they were safely back on the driveway, they almost didn't make it to the house. The ice-shrouded grass in the middle of the drive had been drifted over with loose snow, and more than once the motor lugged and whined before the bumper finally broke through a ridge of snow and the car lurched forward another few feet.

It took ten minutes more to negotiate the rest of driveway, but they finally made it.

Anna was out of the car before Evan killed the engine, before the car had fully stopped.

Evan trembled in the icy blast that roiled through the car as she leaped out. He felt as if all of the air had been yanked from his lungs and replaced with something thicker, something polar, glacial.

'Anna,' he called harshly when he had a second to catch his breath. 'Stop! You wait for me!'

Surprisingly, she did. She stood just to the right of the front door, not moving until Evan stumped up the three steps to the porch, followed by Vera.

The front door was unlocked. Evan turned the knob and pushed the door open.

Inside, the house was pitch black. And it smelled. A musty, rotten smell, like a root cellar that hadn't been aired for decades, like a dark and dank pit with fine hair-like growths of fungus coating the walls and making them spongy to the touch.

Underneath the mustiness lay yet another smell, darker and more pungent. Evan couldn't place it but he knew that he didn't like it at all.

Still, there was no alternative but to step into the darkened hallway. He didn't go far, though. Anna crowded close behind him on the porch, with Vera hanging back an arm's length from the girl.

'Aunt Annie,' he called into the emptiness. 'It's me. Evan. You awake? Aunt Annie?' There was no answer.

Evan reached through for the light plate he figured must be next to the door. His hand slid up and down the wall for a long time, his fingers searching for the switch.

'Damn, where's the light,' he mumbled.

'She doesn't have electricity,' Anna

murmured over his shoulder. 'Remember?'

He stared at the girl. He should have remembered. The whole of Shadow Valley had been electrified nearly a generation before, poles supporting spider-web wires springing up alongside the roads like magic. At farm after farm, in window after window, golden light began to glow at dusk, replacing the uneven flickering of candles or kerosene lamps. Yard lights cast their silvery radiance over barns and sheds and granaries from dusk until dawn. Eventually, the whole valley had glittered through the night like a dim reflection of the overhead sky.

Everywhere but here.

Aunt Annie had steadfastly refused even to let the contractors onto her land. Her place remained dark.

'Bring me the flashlight from the glove compartment,' Evan said to Vera.

She started to say something, then visibly thought better of it and tramped back through the snow to the car. Evan could hear the *click click click* as the hot engine cooled rapidly.

'You two go back to the car and wait there,' Evan said to Anna when Vera handed him the flash.

'No,' Anna said. 'I can't. I've got to go in with you.'

He looked at her, shrugged, nodded, and turned on the flashlight, aiming it into the dark interior of the house. Something scuttled across the carpet and disappeared into the blackness at the end of the entry hall. Evan stepped in.

Anna followed, then Vera.

The doors on the right, the ones that led to Rachel's old parlor, were closed tightly. But the ones on the left were open an inch or two. Evan pulled on one and shivered as the old wood slid away, disappearing into the secret niche within the wall, baring a deep pit of blackness. He flashed the light inside.

Whenever Rachel's daughter had died, it was recently.

The body wasn't discolored, hadn't started to decay. Aunt Annie slumped on the old Victorian sofa, her body so huge that it hardly seemed possible for the couch to support her dead weight. She was swathed in the remains of some ancient gown that hung in grey folds over her body.

Strangely, she seemed peaceful.

Without speaking, Anna walked past Evan. She acted as if she had anticipated the scene before them.

Evan's flashlight caught her outline and flung it onto the wall opposite. The shadow danced and jittered as Evan's hand shook — from cold as much as from shock — until it seemed possessed, demonic.

Anna laid the back of her hand on Aunt Annie's cheek. 'It's cold,' she said, looked back over her shoulder. 'Like ice.'

Evan approached her and gently drew her away from the body. 'Come on, we've got to get home. We'll call from there.'

'Call?'

'The hospital in Burlington. The sheriff. The mortuary. Whoever.'

When they left, they carefully closed the doors to the parlor. Aunt Annie rested for the last time on the sofa in Mattie's parlour, beneath the northern window.

15

Lila sprang from the sofa.

She had known that they would find Annie — *I can't bear to think of that woman as* Aunt *Annie* — that they would find Rachel's reclusive wretch of a daughter dead. The journal had made that clear. She didn't think that the writer would have indulged in any mock-suspense and then reveal that it had all been a dream on Anna's part, some chimerical nightmare concocted, as the story went, of 'undigested bit of beef, a blot of mustard, a crumb of cheese, a fragment of an underdone potato.'

Finding the body presented no surprise.

But Lila had unconsciously expected them to enter the house, traverse the long hallway like a trio of sneak-thieves huddled behind the glare of their flashlight, silently climb the stairs, and make their way to the front-corner bedroom on the south side of the upstairs corridor — to the room that Annie had shared as a child with her mother.

They would have opened the door — it would not have been barred to them as so many doors had been barred to Lila. It would have swung open as silently as they had ascended the stairs, and they would have stepped in and arranged themselves in a respectful line at the edge of a double bed — again, the one shared by Annie and Rachel for so many years.

There they would have found her.

She would look as if she were asleep. However hard her life had been, in Lila's imagination, she would have died quietly, as easily as a single breath might extinguish a guttering candle's flame.

Lila knew where that image had come from.

That was how her own grandmother had died. During her final years, she had been unable to care for herself sufficiently for her to live alone. She had been forced by time and age and circumstances to give up the small house she had lived in all of her adult life and move in with her closest living relative . . . Lila's mother.

Neither her mother nor her grandmother had been happy with the arrangement, but there was no money for a retirement home, nor would Grandma have been willing to live in one.

'Parking lot for the not-yet-dead,' she had said when the subject was first broached. 'Zombies with walkers and zombies with wheelchairs.' She had visited friends in places like that, she had said, her jaw tense with anger and determination, and there was no way on God's Great Green Earth that she would end up there. Better just to have someone blindfold her, take her to the nearest freeway entrance, spin her widdershins three times, and give her a solid push in the right direction. Let the Mack trucks or the oil rigs or the SUVs driven by idiots talking on their cell phones solve the problem.

So she had moved in with her daughter.

And they had proceeded to make life a living hell for each other. Neither could be out of the other's sight for a moment.

One day Mom would call Lila to complain that Grandma followed her everywhere, even into the bathroom; and the next day, Grandma would call to complain that Mom never gave her a moment's peace, not even in the bathroom. If one of them dozed in front of the television, the other one would kick at the sleeper's feet to awaken her, then explain that it was 'Just to make sure that you were all right.'

Nothing was ever cooked quite right. The laundry never smelled quite right or was folded quite right. The dishes were never stacked the right way in the drainer, or put away in the proper cabinet. Whatever one chose to watch on the television in the small living room was automatically *stupid*, but if the other changed channels, she was being demanding and coercive.

Grandma had her own bedroom at Lila's mother's. Friends had brought in her old head- and footboard, her own mattress — as old and swaybacked as it was — her own dresser and night tables, and arranged them so that the room was

174

almost identical to the one in Grandma's old house. They even hung all of her pictures on the wall. None of family, of course, since Lila and her mother were Grandma's family, but landscapes and sentimental scenes of cowboys and farmers and horses and cattle that apparently reminded Grandma of her younger years.

After the first month or so, however, Grandma never used that bedroom. She was too cold in that old bed. Or she was too lonely. Or she couldn't stand the constant draft in the room. Or the room was too stuffy.

Gradually, by an unspoken accord that was perhaps as close as the two women ever came to agreeing on anything, she simply shared Lila's mother's bed. And when she became too feeble to walk on her own   her own private version of a zombie with a walker — it was just easier to settle her down in the master bedroom, with all of her medications right at hand on the night stand.

Lila's mother's bed simply became her own.

And that was where Lila's mother had found her early one morning. When Lila's mother woke at dawn that day, irritated (as always) at the way the sun slanted through the window at just the right angle to strike her eyes (as always) and wake her at that ungodly hour (as always), Grandma was lying next to her, cold, stiff, hours-dead, legs outstretched, feet together, hands straight at her side as if she had been arranged by some ghostly mortician who had crept into the room in the dark of night to perform his ghoulish ministrations.

That was where Lila had seen her, only a short while after her mother had called her around noon to say, 'Grandma passed away last night. The paramedics are just leaving, so if you want to see her before they take her to the funeral home, you better come now.' And then she had hung up.

No explanation of why she had not called earlier. No expression of grief or sorrow. No commiseration with her only daughter . . . now her only relative left on earth.

Nothing.

Lila had never allowed herself to consciously remember much of that day, or of the next, or the next. There were the usual formalities — the trip to the mortuary to make arrangements, although when they arrived they discovered that Grandma had already planned everything out, down to the kind of flowers to be placed on her casket — the one she had ordered almost thirty years before. There was the viewing, which essentially meant sitting in the empty mortuary chapel listening to lachrymose music from a wheezing pipe organ hidden somewhere behind the acres of thick velvet draperies that covered the walls . . . sitting there, unspeaking, next to her mother and waiting long minutes between the few visits from Grandma's old friends and neighbours. There was the funeral — fewer than a dozen people showed up, but the sermon, intoned by a young minister who had never actually met Lila's grandmother, was mercifully short. It concentrated on the standards: 'ashes to ashes, dust to dust, in the sure hope of the resurrection . . . '

And then the interment in the newest part of the newest cemetery in town, where the trees were little more than thumb-thick sticks barely taller than the tombstones and the grass still showed distinct lines where the rolls of turf — what Lila always thought of as *footsie-rolls* — had been laid only weeks or months before.

End of Grandma. End of story. End of memory.

That was why she had been so startled to suddenly realized that she was sitting, not only where Rachel — and after her Annie — had sat to watch the sunsets, but also where Annie had *died*.

She walked away from the sofa, crossing to the far wall. As she passed the fireplace and the portrait of Rachel, she slowed but she did not stop. She did not look up to meet Rachel's eyes. She wasn't sure why.

A short while later, she stepped into the hallway.

The pocket doors in the opposite wall were still shut tight. She looked down the hall. The door at the end of the hall — the kitchens, long since refurbished into a single kitchen and a pantry, according to the journal — were shut. At least no light seeped around where the door should be.

Upstairs, the hall light was dark. Apparently she wasn't needed up there for act two of the *Incredible Sleeping Corpses*.

Come one, come all! Seeing is believing! And Believing is . . .

No, she would not go upstairs. Not yet.

She didn't dare try the front door either. Right now, she didn't want to know if she was locked in or not.

She felt as if she was locked up inside herself.

That was bad enough.

She returned to Mattie's parlour and sat down to read.

16

From the unknown writer's journal:

The next day, an hour or so after the hearse from the Quint Mortuary in Burlington (who had buried Shadow Valley's dead for thirty years) removed the body, Vera came with a couple of other older women who had spent their adult lives wondering about Aunt Annie and her house and what might lie inside.

They were going to 'take care of things,' now that Aunt Annie was finally gone.

For the second time in two days, for only the second time since 1914, someone other than Rachel, Annie, or Grandma entered the house.

The women pushed through the open doors of Mattie's parlor first. The room was immaculate. Whatever else Annie had become in her old age, no one could fault her housekeeping. There was not a speck of dust, not a whisper of dirt. The room was like a museum showpiece. Even the ninety-year old wooden legs of the ornately carved Victorian sofa — now bereft of their weighty burden — gleamed softly in the filtered light.

The doors opposite, opening into what had been Rachel's parlor, were closed and locked. Vera tugged at the knob once or twice and thought she felt the old mechanism inside give, but by unspoken consensus the women filed down the hallway instead and disappeared into the rear of the house.

The kitchen was as sterile as the rest of the house. The table and counters were starkly bare, gleaming in the bright sunlight that cut through clean windows. The cupboard doors were closed tightly. When Vera and the others opened them, they discovered only half a box of crackers tucked in one corner of the far cupboard. In the smaller one to the right of the sink they found a single chipped plate and one ceramic mug.

The drawers were empty as well, except for one table knife, one fork, and one spoon in the silverware drawer. In the next drawer over, they found a long, sharp bread knife and a spoon large enough to serve as a ladle.

Two pots — scrubbed inside and out — sat on the rear of the antique wood-burning stove that had survived the inferno that Rachel had become and had still served her daughter almost three quarters of a century later.

Other than the box of crackers, there was no food in the kitchen. And none in the adjoining pantry, in what had once been Rachel's kitchen.

One bedroom upstairs had been used. The mattress sagged where Annie's bulk had lain on it for so many years. A single wardrobe held two ragged dresses. Two hand-stitched quilts, so old that the material in the patchwork Double Wedding Ring designs had faded to a uniform ecru, lay folded at the foot of the bed. There was no mirror, nothing on the wall except three old prints, unrecognizable faces so washed out by time that they seemed more ghostly memories than pictures.

The other bedrooms were empty. The doors were closed but unlocked. Inside, there was nothing. No carpets, no beds, no wardrobes, no curtains at the age-spotted windows.

Nothing.

That left only one room to explore. Rachel's parlour. Standing before the locked sliding doors, Vera felt a moment's pang. She wasn't sure whether they should try to force it or wait for later, but old Mrs. Hodgfield shouldered past her. Now that Annie was gone, Myrtle Hodgfield was oldest inhabitant of the valley and as stubborn as the mules her husband had bred until one kicked him in the head in 1929 and sent him spinning into a better world.

Better for *her* at least.

With a *humph* she took a knob in each hand and pushed.

The lock gave way so abruptly that Myrtle Hodgfield almost tumbled into the room. The other women were pressing close behind her, Vera leading the pack.

Halfway open, the doors shuddered to a halt. The wood creaked and groaned but the women grabbed the doors and shoved. Whatever had obstructed the doors gave way and the heavy panels slid the rest of the way into the walls with a rustled whispering like dry winter snow blowing over sagebrush on a mountain's shoulder.

The women entered Rachel's parlour.

It stank.

'My lord,' Myrtle Hodgfield muttered, 'what died in here?'

Neither of the other two ventured to speak. The stench was nearly overpowering but somehow it wasn't quite what one would expect of a mouse — or even a good-sized rat — that had expired in the narrow hollows behind the walls, its corpse slowly desiccating and shriveling until nothing remained to generate an odour.

One of the other women — Gilda Pettingale, it was, whose heart would attack her (as the saying went) in her own rocking chair within the year — had once come home from a long vacation to discover that her sitting room reeked worse than the garbage pit out back of the swaybacked barn on their place. She had almost fainted at the first whiff, then stiffened her back and charged inside. No mere *smell* would keep her from having the neatest, the cleanest house in Shadow Valley.

She and her husband — old Elihu, who had a good twenty years on his wife but who, as fate would have it, would survive her by another twenty — searched high and low, probing and poking in every corner of the room, checking behind the antique drapes that pooled across her grandmother's old carpet, even going so far as to remove several ceiling panels to make certain that nothing once-living had curled up there to die. They found nothing, but they were certain that the smell came from the sitting room. The moment they stepped outside its double doors, the rankness faded rapidly away to nothing. From the hallway, there was practically no smell at all.

Finally, in a moment of desperation, old Elihu — handkerchief to his nose and arthritic knees crackling like dried twigs bent too far — knelt in front of the

185

fireplace and began probing with an old rake handle he had found tucked away in the tool shed.

'Gild,' he said without turning to face her. 'Think it's up here. There's something, anyway.'

He tried to continue but after a coughing fit that nearly pitched him into the ashes, he had to struggle to his feet and stagger away from the fireplace for a couple of minutes, partly to catch his breath and partly to clear the fetidness from his lungs before tackling the flue again.

Once more on his knees, his old back arched and twisted so that he was halfway up the flue himself, he began poking and nudging with the handle until . . .

With a shriek that belied both his age and his gender, he suddenly straightened up, striking his shoulders on the brickwork and knocking flecks of dust and soot on the back of his worn denim work shirt.

'Shii-iit!'

'Elihu Pettingale! You know I don't allow . . . '

Her voice tapered off into a tiny

186

whimper as her husband finally extricated himself from the fireplace and backed away, looking oddly humped.

'Get this off of me!' he thundered. To her certain memory, he hadn't yelled so loud for a generation, not since their youngest had finally gotten his man-growth and took off for parts unknown, but between the nauseating reek — which had increased by at least a thousand percent in a matter of seconds — and the thick matter oozing down the back of his shirt, no one could have blamed him.

It took the two of them nearly an hour to clean up what Elihu kept calling the *gaw-dawful* mess and another hour in the tub — and three pots of steaming water from the stove — for him to begin feeling quarter-way human and partway clean again. The sitting room stank like blue blazes for the rest of the day, even with all of the windows open the strong breeze.

Two raccoons had apparently decided that the deep, dark, cool chimney would be a perfect place to build a nest. They hadn't counted on Gilda and Elihu kindling a fire the night before they left on vacation — it had been an unusually cool spring evening, and the fire really felt good as they sat in the sitting room and pored over seed catalogues, planning out the summer's garden — nor had the unfortunately short-sighted raccoons foreseen the extreme difficulty of scrabbling their way up the soot-slick bricks while in a panic, desperate to evade the sudden gouts of heat and smoke.

So they had died in silent agony . . . and quietly rotted away while Gilda and Elihu enjoyed the beauties of Yellowstone Park in the spring, courtesy of that same wild youngest who had turned out to be a fairly sharp stock trader.

But even that, Gilda would have agreed, even that *gawdawful reek* didn't carry the undercurrent of . . . of decay and purulence that permeated Rachel's parlor.

It might not have been as potent as *eau de raccoon* had been but it was subtly worse, more profoundly unsettling.

Gilda made her way to the window, threw back the drapes, and flung open the casement. That helped a bit.

'There, that's better,' she said, breathing deeply of the fresh air.

After a moment, the women turned their attention to the room itself.

The walls were hung with peeling wallpaper in a design not made since the turn of the century. The floor was so littered with papers that none of the women could tell if there was hardwood beneath or carpeting. They could see yellowed newspapers, old circulars advertising products that disappeared before the second World War, crumpled Grange bulletins announcing meetings scheduled for sometime in 1939.

Myrtle Hodgfield took a step toward the center of the room. Beneath the papers stacked up along the wall, something scuttled away.

Myrtle Hodgfield shrieked and jerked back. Her scream — and the sudden backward pressure of her bulk — forced the others to retreat suddenly into the hall.

Vera grunted and muttered under her breath something that might have been, 'Lived on a farm for seventy-eight years and scared of a rat!' had she not been afraid of what Myrtle Hodgfield would say if she had heard. Instead, Vera contented herself with mumbling and stalked into the room, her pride and dignity dented both by Myrtle's preceding her there and because one of the woman had stepped on her toe as well. Vera walked across the papers — gingerly, to be sure — threading her way between tottering stacks, and stopped at the dark oak highboy against the far wall.

It was piled high with boxes. Dozens of boxes. Scores of boxes. Boxes gaudy with satin and ribbon, perhaps once gorgeous in crimson and scarlet and cardinal but now faded and streaked and mottled, diseased-looking and fly-specked. The pile reeked of rotting paper and old glue and something else, heavy and cloying.

Although she had absolutely no desire to touch anything on the highboy, Vera gingerly opened the top box.

Chocolates. Square, round, oblong. The whole box was full of chocolates, with only one piece missing.

'Look at this,' she said to the other two

women, not touching the box but gesturing with her forefinger.

They crowded around, one on each side of Vera as she carefully replaced the box top and wiped her hands on her calico apron.

'Are they all . . . ?' Myrtle's voice shook with more than age.

Vera shrugged. 'I think so.'

She opened another box. One piece missing.

She opened another. Again, a single empty space among the small paper wrappings.

'Why would she . . . '

She began tossing covers right and left, ignoring her earlier distaste, pawing through the stacks of boxes.

Boxes of chocolates — pound boxes, it looked like — all of them missing one single piece.

She noticed what looked like tiny teeth marks scratched across some — mice, she thought, and shuddered at the thought of vermin running freely across a parlor highboy. But most of the candies were untouched even though they had turned chalky with age and some were dried and melted and crumbling into the boxes.

She turned and stared at the other women.

Then she turned back and began counting the boxes, one by one.

There were seventy gaudy Valentine's Day boxes. And seventy pieces of chocolate missing. No more. No less.

'Vera,' said Myrtle Hodgfield, her voice little more than a whisper. 'Look at this.'

She held out a small piece of thick paper — once white but now yellowed with age, faded until the thin border of red roses seemed like little more than a ghost. It was perhaps three inches long and an inch-and-a-half wide. Something was written on it in the beautiful, almost calligraphic handwriting of another century.

'It was still tied to the first box you opened, the one on top.'

Warily, Vera took the bit of paper. She had to study it to read the faded writing.

'For my beloved Annie. Mine always.'

Vera stared at the tag. *For my beloved Annie.* Who in the world would have sent

Aunt Annie something like that?

'Look at the back,' Myrtle urged.

Vera turned the card over. Something was written there, also, in a different script, one less studied, less professional-looking than the first. The lines seemed slightly shaky.

'This was the last box of candy Johnnie sent me before he died in the War.'

Vera looked startled.

'Annie kept this that long? Since the War?'

In Shadow Valley, *The War* universally meant World War II, not any of the subsequent conflicts, even though each of them has cost the valley in young men's blood.

Myrtle shook her head. Her eyes were wide with disbelief.

'No, dear. I'm pretty sure that *Johnnie* was John Redmond, you remember the Redmonds, Alma and Roger, they moved away . . . oh, fifteen, twenty years ago.'

Vera nodded. 'But they didn't have a son . . . '

'No, they didn't. John Redmond wasn't their son. John Redmond was

Roger's *uncle*. He died at the age of nineteen . . . in *World War I*.'

Without another word, the women replaced the boxes on the highboy, leaving them looking as untouched as they had when the women entered Rachel's parlour.

In the drawers underneath the candy boxes lay other boxes, most of them tattered old shoe boxes without lids, each filled with old photographs and prints, most of them probably family portraits although no one present could identify any of the faces.

The women gingerly carried the boxes of pictures out to the backyard and burned them in the incinerator that had sat unused behind the shed for who knew how many years.

Then they made additional trips with bundles of papers removed from the floor.

They burned the half-box of crackers.

But Vera stacked the boxes of chocolate neatly in one corner.

Later, when asked why she had done something so obviously odd, Vera couldn't explain.

17

Shaken by what she had just read, Lila closed the journal and rested it in her lap.

This was the last box of candy Johnnie sent me before he died in the War.

The journal's writer had not added any dates to the entries, but Lila had been assuming that the last events she had read about — Annie's death and burial — had to have been from the 1970s or 1980s. Certainly no earlier than the late 1960s.

Before he died in the War.

World War I.

Annie had never married. That much was clear from the journal. She had never had the chance to escape Rachel's anger and hatred and frustration. She had been caught in Rachel's web, twisted through years of what the two of them must have perceived as deprivation while Mattie and her children received more and more and more.

Rachel must have taught Annie well.

Must have filled her and over-filled her with venom.

Yet . . .

This was the last box of candy Johnnie sent me before he died in the War.

Had Annie had a chance, this single chance, to escape?

Johnnie.

John Redmond.

Lila closed her eyes.

She could almost imagine what young John Redmond might have looked like, first as a boy in his late teens, perhaps in one of those stiffly formal portraits from the early 1900s. White, high-collared shirt buttoned to the throat. Sunday-go-to-meeting jacket buttoned just as tightly, as if trying to restrain the sheer energy and enthusiasm and unfettered love of life that would have given the boy so much of his appeal. Perhaps posed with his favorite companion, his dog, probably what Lila's grandmother would have called a *Heinz dog* — fifty-seven varieties all mixed together to create a single unique breed — its front paws outstretched as it lay proudly yet dutifully next to its lord and master.

Later, around 1917 or 1918, he might have been photographed in his uniform: his stiff-brimmed hat — *Smokey-bear hat* to younger generations — square on his head, his uniform jacket of some coarse, nondescript material stretched tautly across his chest as he posed, his puttees tied around his ankles and calves to protect them. Perhaps he had sent Annie a photograph along with the box of chocolates — *'For my beloved Annie. Mine always'* — two small gifts to remind her of him while he was away, to help her remember what he looked like until he returned.

Which he never did.

Lila could feel the heartbreak in that hand-written note on the back of the gift-tag.

And the *horror* of the rest of the boxes, stacked neatly on the highboy, gathering dust year after year, ignored after Annie had helped herself to her single piece.

One single piece of smooth, dark, rich chocolate, caramel-filled or nougat or fruit-mix, it didn't matter. What mattered was the first gush of sweetness in her mouth to remind her of . . . of what? Of a first kiss stolen on a warm spring evening under the box elders, far from Rachel's watchful eye? Of something more?

What mattered was the memory.

Eat this in remembrance of him.

Lila shuddered.

Some things should not have to be borne, *could not be* borne.

Her hand still on the journal, she leaned back and closed her eyes. She had no idea how late it was, nor did she want to look at her cell. It would no doubt still read twelve o'clock midnight and zero seconds.

It felt *late*. That time of night when energy ebbs and the body flags, when statistics tell us that death stalks the final-care wings of hospitals in shadowed secrecy, unstoppable, seeking its next victims. Her eyes felt red and watery and her fingers trembled slightly where they rested on the journal.

Oh, how she wished she could rest them, just close them and let herself be carried away by sleep . . .

Except that she was certain that Rachel, or Annie, or the house itself would visit her with angry dreams if she tried to escape them even for a moment.

But they couldn't stop her from closing her eyes and thinking. Remembering.

Remembering her own slyly stolen first kiss so many long and lonesome years before.

His name had been Rob, and he was young and handsome — *beautiful*, actually would have been more precise, she realized — with soft grey eyes and dark wavy hair, with strong hands and arms, and a body sculpted by swimming and running.

She had fallen for him at first sight. Fallen hard. She had been . . . what, sixteen or seventeen. There had been other infatuations before Rob, to be sure, but he had been the first time that she *knew* it was love and that it would last forever.

Forever!

One short month would be more accurate. At first, there had been long, languorous looks exchanged across the intervening desks in study hall, two sets of eyes disguising their true intent behind strategically propped books — she had found that thick, word-bound history books worked the best, because they could stand by themselves and allow busy hands to scrawl love-knots and heart-linked initials on random bits of paper.

Then there were the quick, bitter-sweet snatches of conversation in crowded hallways, standing beside his locker or hers and pretending, for the benefit of friends nearby who otherwise might gossip and spread the word — or tease unmercifully — that they were merely exchanging the latest English assignment or comparing results from the last pop-quiz old man Heberer had thrown at them in Algebra that morning. Anything to keep people from talking, because otherwise word might get back to Lila's mother — Lila's *strange* mother, whom none of her school friends felt comfortable being around — about who her little girl was spending time with.

Only once did Rob come by her house, early one evening, almost shyly knocking on the door and casually introducing himself.

'Hello, Mrs. Ellis. I'm Rob. Rob Garner. I'm in Lila's . . . uh . . . English class, and I wondered if she's home. I need a little help with this story we're reading and since she's so good with literature and stuff, I hoped . . . '

He trailed off as if fearful of simply babbling on and on until Lila's mother lost patience and slammed the door in his face.

She didn't slam the door. But she did glare at him as if he were some kind of walking disease about to infect her premises before she called over her shoulder, 'Lila, there's a boy here to see you.' Her voice was harsh.

Boy!

Rob might be only seventeen but he was a *man* in Lila's eyes.

She had come running down the hall, slowing just in time to keep her mother from noticing how excited she was.

'Thanks, Mom. Oh, hi, Rob' — so *offhand*, so *nonchalant*. 'How are you?'

'Uh . . . okay. Thanks.'

There had been a moment of strained silence, then Lila's mother had backed wordlessly away, finally disappearing into the kitchen.

'I wanted to ask you,' Rob said, his voice intentionally pitched louder than needed, primarily so that it would carry into the kitchen. 'Were we supposed to read all the way to page 100 or just the first chapter? I don't remember and I know you take good notes.' He winked, slowly, and her heart nearly stopped. When he grinned, she grinned back so widely that she was afraid her head might split in two . . . now *that* would be gross!

'Um, all the way to 100, I think.'

'You mean, *go all the way* . . . to the end?'

Lila had blushed furiously.

They had carried on like that for a few minutes, tossing throw-away lines back and forth through the doorway, all the time half-listening to the clatter of pots and pans from the kitchen as Lila's mother prepared dinner.

And all the time they had been drawing closer and closer to each other, their feet

202

resolutely on opposite sides of the threshold but their upper bodies straining to touch.

'Well, thanks again, Lila,' Rob finally said, his lips so close to hers that she could taste the crisp, minty cleanness of his breath and draw his masculine scent into herself through her nose.

'You're . . . welcome . . . Rob.' It was all she could do to speak. His eyes were getting deeper, darker, beginning to envelop her. She wasn't sure how much longer she would be able to breathe.

Their lips touched, softly, almost chastely, but it was still more than she could bear, more than she should have to bear . . .

Because — 'Lila Anne Ellis! You get in this house this instant!'

Technically, she was already *in* the house, but Lila knew immediately what her mother had meant, and without thinking a further thought she drew herself into the entry and closed the door . . . she might even have *slammed* the door, so startled and frightened and embarrassed was she.

She didn't even get to see the look in Rob's eyes after they kissed, or look longingly at his lips, or watch him saunter down the walk after the door was closed . . . things she spent long hours imagining for weeks, months after he had stopped talking to her, stopped even noticing her in the halls or in classes at school.

'What were you thinking, girl?' Lila's mother had thundered at her. 'Standing on my very doorstep and *kissing* that boy? Who is he anyway? How long have you two been carrying on like that? What else have you . . . ?'

It went on and on all night.

Lila's mother didn't like Rob's hair — it was too long and greasy and you couldn't trust boys who wore their hair that long and didn't even *try* to keep it clean. She didn't like the way he had spoken to her — he was too smart-mouthed by half, with his pretending to have come by *just* . . . *just* to check on homework. Yes, yes, and butter wouldn't but melt in *his* mouth, would it? She didn't like his clothes — his pants were far too tight and dragged far too low across his hips; she knew what he was advertising, oh yes, no one could miss what he wanted. And that T-shirt of his with that obscene message . . .

It had just been an old Dead Kennedys shirt, so faded that the logo was barely visible, its background black little more than washed-out grey.

Lila had tried to point this out to her mother.

'That's right. Filthy! And ragged and torn. And no sleeves. I know what he was advertising with his shirt torn that way, bunching his muscles up like he was . . . '

And on and on and on.

The next day came the first of many telephone calls from Lila's grandmother.

What was that old line from the camp song: 'Second verse, same as the first, A little bit louder and a little bit worse.'

That described her grandmother's calls.

There were no boys for a long time after that.

It hurt too much even to think about it. Lila was sure that the few other boys that she knew were now looking at her . . . strangely. When she turned her head — and sometimes even when she didn't — they whispered to each other and sniggered. None of them spoke to her in the halls. None stopped by her locker to exchange assignments.

No, there were no boys for a long, *long* time.

And no kisses, and no . . .

Nothing.

Lila sighed and stood.

She walked over to the lithograph of Rachel and glared pointedly at it for a few moments, then turned and left Mattie's parlour

She did not even look at the doors leading into the room across the hallway . . . that would have been Rachel's parlour, the room where the women had found . . .

She sniffed.

Yes, the air was scented with chocolate, but suddenly Lila discovered that she found the scent repellent.

She made her way to the stairs and ascended to the second floor. The hall light was still out. She felt along the wall until she found the switch and placed her hand firmly over it.

No more nasties, Rachel, she thought, and flicked the switch.

The light glowed, perhaps not as brightly as it had before but enough for her to see the six doors lining the hallway. They appeared tightly closed.

She went to the nearest one, the first on her left. She had not yet seen the inside of that room. She tried the knob. It was locked. It felt as immoveable as the others had when she first tried them.

No more nasties, Rachel, she insisted mentally as she moved up the hallway to the second door. The old-fashioned bedroom.

She gave the knob a twist.

The door opened.

She pushed it until she could see into the room.

The one-time bedroom was dark but there was enough light from the hall for her to see that it was empty. Completely empty. And it smelled stale, as if years had passed since anyone — herself included — had entered it. The bed was gone, as were the wardrobe and the treadle machine. The picture of Rachel now hung in Mattie's parlor. At least it had stopped levitating and wandering the halls.

She left the door open as she moved to the next door, the one in the front corner above the . . . above *Rachel's* parlour.

Locked. Immoveable.

That left the three doors on the other side of the hall.

'No more nasties, Rachel,' she said aloud. Her voice echoed down the hall. She was pleased to notice that it was strong and vibrant. 'No more. I'm warning you.'

She tried the first one.

The door opened. And the room was empty.

The door to the next room opened as well, so easily and smoothly that it was hard to believe that it had *ever* been locked. And the room was empty.

The final door opened, and that room was empty as well.

Whatever purpose the bodies on the

beds had been intended to serve had apparently been fulfilled.

Lila turned away from the last room. Four of the six doors stood open, the exposed rooms dark and silent and empty. She felt a curious sense of accomplishment. She almost brushed her hands together, as she would have done had she just completed a difficult, dirty, unpleasant, but totally necessary task.

She went back downstairs and resumed her place on the parlor sofa, picked up the book — and mentally daring Rachel and Annie to do their worst — continued reading.

Annie had died. Rachel was dead and gone.

The worst was over.

18

From the unknown writer's journal:

Aunt Annie stayed in the Burlington mortuary for two days.

Evan arranged to have the body returned to Shadow Valley on the afternoon before the funeral and set up in Mattie's parlour. It wasn't much of a viewing by the usual Shadow Valley standards but a few people came, more out of curiosity than anything else. Probably many more stayed away out of a lingering fear. It is hard to overcome the effect of decades of midnight stories and half-heard whisperings.

Evan was there, of course, with Vera and Anna. Anna said very little to anyone. She sat on a hard-backed wooden chair just to the left of the fireplace and stared, perhaps at the monstrous dark oak coffin on a bier in the middle of the room, perhaps somewhere into her own secret nightmares.

About five o'clock, when it became apparent that no one else from the valley was likely to come by, Evan and Vera decided it was time to go home. Anna asked to wait there for a while. After all, Aunt Annie had been her last remaining relative in Grandma's family (except for me, of course).

'Well, dear. I guess a few more minutes won't matter,' Vera said. 'But really, not much more than that. I have dinner to prepare, you know, and Uncle Evan has his chores. We might be willing to wait a bit, but you know the cows won't. They will want their milking right on schedule.'

Anna looked at her as if she had been speaking some arcane dialect of Latvian.

'Evan? Something's wrong . . . ' Aunt Vera seemed unaccountably frightened.

Evan knelt in front of the girl and took her hand in his. She seemed cold, too cold for the heat of the room.

'Anna,' he said gently. 'Anna, honey.'

He waited for her to focus on him.

'Honey, we've gotta go pretty soon. I'm

sure Aunt Annie would have appreciated all the time you've spent here with her today, but we've got to get back to . . . '

'Let me stay.'

That took Evan by surprise

'What? You don't mean that, do you? You don't really want to be here in this big old house, alone with . . . ' His voice trailed off. He didn't want to say *body* or *corpse* or *remains*. Certainly not *stiff*.

'Yes. I do. I do want to be here with her.' Anna straightened and looked right into Evan's eyes. 'I'll be all right. Nobody will want to come out here tonight, and anyway nobody would *dare*.' She laughed, a tight little laugh that was deeply unsettling to both Evan and Vera.

'Vera? What do you think?'

But before Vera could answer, Anna stood and, still holding Evan by the hand, led him — Vera following vacantly, like a patient calf follows its mother — into the hall where their winter things hung on a tall oak rack next to the front door.

'I'll be all right. Really.'

Evan half expected her to follow up with *And thanks for coming to the* viewing. *My, didn't she look like herself?*. *Didn't she look* natural?

She didn't, though. Instead, she simply stood with the front door ajar, mindless of the chilling draft that swirled around them, until they had finished putting on coats, scarves, gloves, and hats, then opened it fully so they could pass through.

And closed it silently behind them.

She had asked to stay there alone.

They let her.

And they would grieve for that choice forever.

With the doors to Mattie's parlor securely closed, Anna watched through the window as the couple drove off, quickly swallowed by the twilight that falls so rapidly and so early in winter. Then she moved to the sofa.

She sat there, cuddled by old, scratchy cushions, while the January night closed in more deeply. She sat, unmoving.

Evening passed into night. About nine o'clock, she stood and crossed the room, perhaps trailing one hand across the polished surface of the closed casket. She opened the doors into the hallway. Icy air billowed around her from the unheated hall. Then she closed the doors behind her, crossed over, and opened the doors into Rachel's parlour.

It was dark inside the room, and bitterly cold, but Anna didn't notice. She walked around the parlour, touching the ragged wallpaper, fingering the hand-made oak mantelpiece meticulously carved decades before by Great-granddad for his youngest wife. The time-faded lithograph of Rachel — young but dour and stern, almost forbidding — glowered from above the fireplace.

The women had cleaned out most of the papers, burning them indiscriminately, but Anna could still see movement along the floorboards as mice — no, she decided, as *rats* scuttled about, searching vainly for their old hiding places. In spite of the comings and goings of the past days, the place smelled musty and dead.

Anna walked completely around the room. She studied every detail of the wainscoting, every angle and curve of the carvings on the highboy, every polished surface of the heavy oak table in the center of the room.

Then she walked to the far wall, to the highboy still laden with faded and decrepit candy boxes. She lifted up the top box of chocolates, crushing a faded satin bow as she tore off the cover. She took a single piece of the candy and, as if not noticing its dusting of white mould or the scratches on its top surface, placed it into her mouth.

She bit down.

The candy tasted . . . heavy, chalky, dark with secrets. The soft centre had crystallized long before and crunched audibly as she chewed. Her throat rasped, suddenly dry and tight, then something in the chocolate registered in her brain and her saliva flowered, swirling around the crumbling stuff, drenching it and making it creamy and rich and thick again.

She heard a noise . . .

She stopped chewing, the open box hanging at a precipitous angle from her hand.

She listened.

Nothing.

She straightened the box just before half a dozen of the pieces threatened to fall out. She took another piece, another, then three at a time, barely stopping to chew or taste, swallowing them as if they were life-giving breath itself.

Without a hint of warning, the double doors into Mattie's parlour slid open. Anna barely noticed until she heard the odd sound again and turned.

The coffin in the centre of the room was still closed. But filaments of light floated above it, glimmered in the darkness of Mattie's parlour, then spun through the air, across the hallway, and into Rachel's parlour. Anna watched entranced, a thin dribble of chocolate staining her chin.

The filaments continued to spin into Rachel's parlor.

And now the coffin *was* moving, a faint vibration, not quite a flutter of the heavy wood, but enough.

Anna opened her mouth to scream. Her teeth were stained brown with melted chocolate.

The filaments swirled faster, stifling her

scream as they solidified and swirled into a column, a pillar, a form, vague at first but rapidly taking shape. More and more light filaments sped from the coffin, as if the dead and polished wood were giving up its own essence to create . . . something else.

Rachel.

She stood imperious, eyes three quarters of a century dead and long since rotted into dust still blazing crimson, desiccated lips — no longer even slightly delicious and desirable — curled over rotted teeth, one skeletal hand pointing meaningfully toward Anna.

And then she . . . it . . . was Annie, not yet bloated beyond the human. Still slender, beautiful. As she had been just before Rachel's horrible death.

Then it was Rachel again.

Annie.

Rachel.

Each time it spun through an identity, it became sharper, more explicitly defined. Even through her terror, Anna could see the long, tapered fingernails descending from each fingertip. She could see each hair on the hideous apparition's head as it shifted faster and faster.

She could see the eyes.

The eyes!

Annie. Rachel. Annie Rachel AnnieR-achelannie*rachel* . . .

It moved toward Anna. It reached for her, and the illusion shattered, and Rachel and Aunt Annie dissolved into something else, something hideous, com-posed of rotting cloth like funeral shrouds, and blood-sodden bones, and black decaying flesh, and teeth like fire-blackened stumps, and *things* that moved in and out, around the bones, beneath the tattered clothing. When something like a rat — but larger, with eyes like embers — crawled out of the mouth and sat perched on the remnants of a jaw, Anna screamed and fell to the floor, senseless.

19

Lila flung the journal away from her. It hit the heavy velvet curtains squarely where the window would be but, because of the thickness of the drapes, it did not shatter the glass. Instead it hung for a fraction of a second, its covers spread open as if it were some gigantic angular moth vainly clutching at the fabric, then it tumbled to rest on the folds of drapery pooling on the floor.

Lila stared at it, her eyes narrowed, her cheeks flushed and her breathing rapid.

Liar! Idiotic, sadistic, liar!

After weaving such a story — such a gut-wrenching story in places, heart-wrenching in others — he (*yes, surely, it had to have been a HE to have constructed such a texture of lies, so understanding at first, so sympathetic, then this . . . this . . . .*) had stooped to trickery, to deceit.

To lying.

Rachel had been real, Lila was sure of that. Rachel and Mattie and the repulsive, unnamed and unnamable Great-granddad, and all of the other bit players in this little farce, even Annie herself was real. And there may at one time have been an Evan and Vera (last name unknown) who scrabbled out a miserable livelihood on some featureless farm in the outer reaches of Shadow Valley. And, yes, to be fair, they may even have taken in a poor orphan relative to care for.

But *this* . . .

This abomination!

Lila rose to her feet with a single motion and stalked to the fireplace. Again she glared at the lithograph of Rachel, as if daring the long-dead woman to reappear and reveal the truth . . . the *TRUTH* . . . not this tissue of perverted fantasy . . . the Truth about what had happened to Anna that night in this misbegotten house!

The chandelier light dimmed, brightened, dimmed again and stayed that way, thrusting Mattie's parlour into shadows. Lila whirled around as, behind her, the light illuminating the hallway also dimmed, brightened, dimmed . . . and then winked out. Somewhere down the hall, though, another light remained because a thin glow reflected from the wainscoting and floor panels, as if they were a feeble invitation for Lila to follow.

The Light. The Light. Come, follow the Light.

She did.

Without glancing back at Rachel — *may she rest forever in whatever nameless Hell was created just for her* — Lila left the parlour yet one more time, made her way down and hall and up the stairs. At the top she stopped. All of the doors were closed again. The upstairs light was out as well, so the hall itself seemed little more than a long shaft of impenetrable darkness, stretching from blackness behind her to an infinity of blackness in front of her.

Except.

Except one small spot of light, infinitesimally small in the darkness around her. But it glowed all the brighter for the contrast.

For a moment, she could not place it.

They she realized that it must be that most common of things in late nineteenth-century houses . . . a keyhole, bored through the brass plate and the wooden core of the door, and a waiting receptacle for one of those huge, heavy keys. The kind people sometimes called *skeleton keys*. Except — *wasn't there always an* EXCEPT *in this godforsaken house* — except none of the other interior doors had had keyholes. Or they had been stopped up, because even with lights on inside, no light had shown through.

She didn't, of course, have any keys at all, skeleton or otherwise. But she stepped to the door anyway.

It was what she had come to think of as door number three.

Number One was the front corner room on the left, where Rachel and Annie had slept. Number Two was the room with the here-now-gone-the-next-second bedroom suite. So this one was Room Number Three — previously locked and barred to her.

She reached toward the door, found the

knob by guesswork — it should be just above where a key would be inserted — and turned it.

No key required.

The door swung fully open at her lightest touch. It was clearly an invitation.

But from whom . . .?

She stepped inside.

The room was almost empty. The walls looked as if they had never been properly papered. In fact, as she studied them more closely, she realized that what she had for an instant taken to be tattered remains of some yellow-brown monstrosity of a print, sprinkled over with tiny black marks like insect trails was in fact . . . newspaper.

This was one of Rachel's unneeded bedrooms. She might have refused to let Mattie encroach onto her side of the house, but Mattie (Lila would have been willing to bet nearly anything) had gotten her revenge in the end. Lila could almost hear the exchanges, Mattie, all sweetness and light, whispering into the old goat's ear.

'But, dear, we really don't have the

money to finish off that bedroom right now. Young Edmond desperately needs shoes . . . '

Or:

'But my sweet, if we spend that much on wall paper for a room that no one is using, poor Albert will have to wear that ragged coat for yet another winter, and signs point to a heavy snow ahead . . . '

One excuse after another, perhaps communicated as pillow-talk just after Mattie and the execrable old Great-granddad had finished . . . whatever he found pleasurable with her on the old high-boarded oak bedstead in bedroom Number Six.

And Rachel would have to settle for newsprint for yet another year, and then another, and another. And finally the room would remain as it had always been, the thin paper vibrating harshly when winter storms attached the unprotected corner of the house, then growing stiffer and more fragile as the summer heat baked it, and finally tearing in long tendrils with the subtle movements of the old house's foundations.

The window was actually boarded over. Lila had no idea when the last person had peered through the glass at the landscape outside. Rust marks trailed down the boards like so many rivulets of dried blood, so the nails were undoubtedly old and corroded with age, with the mustiness of an unused room, with the damps of winter and the minor drips of summer storms.

The only piece of furniture stood in the centre. Lila would have been willing to bet that if she had had a tape measure, she would have discovered that it stood in the *exact* centre of the room.

It was an odd-looking structure. It had a single support, apparently carved from a three-inch-thick round of oak, rising out of four equally ornately carved feet, each ending with a lion-claw-and-ball motif popular a century ago. At the top of the support was a large desk-like arrangement, although it was not angled as she might have expected, something like an architect's table. Instead it was flat — and again she was certain that it was *perfectly* flat — and rimmed with a narrow band of decorative wood.

It held one item.

Lila couldn't be certain from a distance, but it looked like another Bible. Not a small personal bible like the one in the bookcase downstairs, but one of those huge, monolithic old Family Bibles, with cover-boards a quarter of an inch thick, encased in tooled and gilded leather.

It was the kind of Bible a couple might have received a century or so ago, if all of their relatives had pooled their resources and purchased a copy to celebrate their wedding. And it was the kind intended to last for generations, with scores of pages at the front and the back left empty to serve as durable and enduring family histories.

She was half afraid, half excited to see what this book contained.

If nothing else, she was about to discover the name of Great-granddad. That would be a relief. At least she would have a name to attach to the old goat when she cursed him under her breath.

She drew nearer.

The book was already open. Nearly all of the pages lay on the left side of the gutter. Not one fluttered.

Only a handful remained unturned on the right side. The end of the story.

20

Her fingers didn't exactly tremble as she reached out toward the Bible, but she felt an unaccountable trepidation.

There was information here, she was sure, information that would be central to her understanding many of the things that had happened to her over the past few hours. It would unravel the mysteries that were Rachel and Annie . . . and now Anna. And perhaps more mysteries that Lila did not even know about yet.

But — and here she shivered — it might also touch *her*. She was in this house, reading that damnable journal, undergoing eldritch events so far out of her normal experience that she didn't even have names to call them by . . . and she was here for a purpose.

That much she knew.

What the purpose *was* . . . well, perhaps that was the question of the night.

She touched the open page.

The paper felt thick and rich beneath her fingertip, more like parchment than the cheap stuff one found in books nowadays, certainly more so than the nearly transparent tissue paper in most of the Bibles she had ever seen. It was finely textured and must once have been a lovely cream colour although age and time had given it a distinctly yellow, jaundiced cast. Even so, the page remained attractive enough and, given its apparent age, in excellent condition.

It was bordered by a profusion of decorations — archaic-looking flowers of no particular taxonomic variety, surrounded and often surmounted by mounds of finely cross-hatched leaves that left the illusion of three-dimensional depth; swirls and arabesques that had a faintly Celtic cast without being legitimately so; faded washes of color that were just enough altered by the passing decades that they seemed to have little to do with the shapes and figures that contained them; fragments of gilding here and there that made the page seem to glow in the dim light.

The page itself was large, perhaps fourteen or fifteen inches across and nearly eighteen inches tall, but the actual space left for writing seemed small since the ornamental border was several inches thick on each side. The effect was of lushness, of purposefully conspicuous consumption (to borrow a term from another decade) — as if the book intended to say, *Here I am. If you can afford me, you can afford my affectations. I might contain the Word of God, but that is less in the sight of men than the beauties and wonders of my workmanship and craftsmanship. Look on me and be awed.*

Lila was not awed.

In spite of the limits set by its framework, the page seemed expansive because it was almost empty. There, where there was room enough for dozens of entries of marriages, of births and deaths, of the varied minutiæ that families might consider important to have recorded for their descendants, there were only two items.

First, the marriage of Obadiah Stevenson to Rachel . . . surname unknown.

Obadiah, Lila thought. *Appropriate. I wonder if anyone ever had the guts to call him O-bad! Not likely!*

So she had a name for Great-granddad, but not for Rachel.

'Surname unknown.'

Lila tried to imagine the consternation when Great-granddad Obadiah had suddenly appeared at the old homestead, with a new — and fourth — wife in tow, her name already officially Rachel *Stevenson*. And neither of them had ever revealed her last name.

Had Obadiah himself known it?

Lila allowed her eyes to shift down the page to the second entry: from that marriage came — following the several miscarriages mentioned in the journal — a single child: Annie Stevenson.

Aunt Annie.

All right. Except for Great-granddad's name, nothing new.

Lila thumbed the page, intending to turn it. Nothing happened. In spite of the fact that she could clearly see the gilded edges of a number of pages between this one and the leather-covered back cover, she could not turn the page.

She touched her tongue to her forefinger and thumb, moistening them lightly, and tried again.

The page did not move. It was as if it had been glued in place . . . as if whoever had set the Bible here for her to look at did not want her to read any further. Or perhaps there was nothing more to read. Obadiah married Rachel of the unknown surname and begat Annie, who begat . . . no one. End of the story. End of the line, for Rachel at least.

Lila tried the preceding page. The verso side of the leaf, curving from the gutter over the rest of the massive volume, was blank, without any decorations. It was simply an unmarked sheet staring up at the light.

Yet when she touched the upper corner with her forefinger, it moved. The leaf slid easily and silently across, covering Rachel's page.

It was as ornamented as the other page had been, although with slightly different flowers, slightly different swirls and flourishes. It too carried the name of Obadiah Stevenson, but here he was listed as marrying one Ethel Pickering. And beneath that entry came the names of five children, three boys and two girls.

Beyond that, nothing. No record of the children marrying, having children of their own, dying. Lila remembered the journal had mentioning that two of Obadiah's wives had moved to Canada and had ultimately lost touch with the old man and his two remaining wives. Apparently whoever was tasked with keeping up the family records — Annie, perhaps — did not care to make any effort to track down the lost half-cousins.

Lila tried the next page.

It, too, turned easily. It, too, was highly ornamented, like but not quite identical to the previous two.

And it, too, carried the name *Obadiah Stevenson*, coupled with that of Naomi Winter. Beneath that, the names of four more children, three girls and ... finally ... one boy to carry on the family name. But there, next to the boy's name, were three additional letters: 'd.s.p.' Lila knew what they meant: '*descessit sine prole*' — died without issue. The boy, whose name was Ennis and who had died at the age of twenty-two, had had no children. The family name had not continued with him.

Other than that, however, there was no indication of what happened to him or to the others. Perhaps they, too, had died young. It happened back then. Families with a dozen children born to a single mother often considered themselves lucky if half of them survived past the age of ten. The dangers were too great — diseases for which there were no medical treatments . . . or for which the medical treatments were in fact more deadly than the illnesses; injuries that led to unstoppable infections and long, lingering, and painful deaths; accidents inherent to frontier living, not excepting attacks by native activists determined to exterminate interlopers on the lands of their heritage.

And for those few to survive to adulthood and marry and propagate . . .

No, there were too many possibilities to name.

And even if the three girls had beaten the odds, there would be no *Stevenson* children among them.

That left only Mattie's family.

Lila knew that that information had to be inscribed on the next sheet.

She reached out and brushed her fingertips on the corner of the left-hand page.

It did not move.

'No!' she yelped, then: 'No. No.'

It was the ultimate disappointment, to be so close to . . . to answers, to comprehension.

'No, Rachel. You can't do this to me. Not now. Not after . . . '

With a resounding, thunderous crash, the front portion of the book swung ponderously over and cracked against the back few pages. It nearly caught Lila's hand as it fell. Dust billowed out, nearly choking her.

Okay, I get the message. Be content with what is offered or I get . . . nothing.

She backed away from the book. The

dim light caught mockingly in the gilt lettering on the front — *HOLY BIBLE* — tossing its reflection back and forth across the deeply incised scrollwork that nearly covered the entirety of the binding.

She backed out of the room and watched the door slowly swing shut. She didn't test to see if it had locked. She knew that she was wanted elsewhere.

21

From the unknown writer's journal:

They found her there at midnight. Evan and Vera came for her, suddenly worried that she might be in danger . . . in mortal peril. They drove out and rushed in through the wide-open doorway, Evan's flashlight flickering like a ghost on the wainscoting of the entry hall.

Anna was sitting stiffly where they had left her, in the Victorian sofa beneath the window in Mattie's parlour. Everything else was as it had been.

Almost.

Aunt Annie's casket lay open, its rose satin lining a blood-like stain in the brightness.

Her body, thin to the point of emaciation, lay stretched on the oak table in Rachel's parlour.

The withered lips were crusted with

something rich and brown and creamy. A rat perched on the body nibbled at the sweetness of the lips.

Vera screamed.

22

Lila snapped the book closed but this time did not throw it. She did not set it down beside her, either, or let it rest in her lap. She merely held it.

Cheap melodrama. Impossible to believe. Certainly nothing important enough to force her back downstairs to read this . . . this drivel. Rats! Magical chocolates!

And yet she knew that she could smell the scent of the chocolates, almost taste its sweetness on her own lips.

It was back again. The scent had almost disappeared for a while, but it had returned, cloying and haunting against the sterility of the house.

She opened the book.

23

From the unknown writer's journal:

Anna seemed to be in shock but she recovered quickly.

She could remember nothing, she told them after the funeral. She could remember only sitting on Aunt Annie's sofa, thinking. And then she must have slept.

She wasn't surprised when the lawyers from Burlington told her about the will. A rather nice estate, including the house with two parlours and the farm itself, along with a tidy sum of money no one in the valley ever suspected Annie to have saved..

Against the strenuous objections of both Evan and Vera, Anna moved into the house within the month.

That was what finally brought me home again.

Evan and Vera were worried. They hadn't seen Anna at all since the move. It had been four months, and they were now more than worried.

I drove out to Anna's the afternoon I arrived.

Even though there was still no telephone in the house — and still no electricity, for that matter — she knew I was coming. She met me on the porch and invited me in to sit in Mattie's parlour. She looked well enough but had put on weight since I had seen her last — not too much, not yet, but still it was there.

We talked for a while, a desultory conversation that carefully skirted anything important. Then she leaned over and touched my knee.

'We're the last, aren't we? The last of Rachel's line.'

'No,' I said. 'We're not even related to Rachel. She was only Grandma's . . . '

Anna cut me off with a quick gesture.

'I'm going to live here, you know,' she said, with a vehemence that startled me. 'I'm going to live here forever, and never want for anything, and have my own parlour.'

And then she leaned even closer, her breath hot and fetid in my face, and with a conspiratorial smile that chilled me and sent my head spinning, she told me what had happened on the night she stayed alone with Aunt Annie's body.

When she finished, she sat back, her eyes sparkling with a vicious delight that still haunts me. I stared. What she had told me was beyond belief, and yet I believed it.

She shivered once, then shook her head as if to clear it, and then she was Anna again, young and beautiful and innocent.

She stood up abruptly.

'Goodbye,' she said, holding out her hand in a gesture that struck me as curiously old-fashioned. And then I understood that she was saying goodbye forever. I would not be welcome in that house again.

'Anna,' I began.

'No,' she said sharply. 'And don't try to talk about what you've heard. We're Family, they're outsiders. Family keeps its secrets.'

She laughed, a hideous and frightening

laugh that seemed to come from a body much larger than hers, much older and more acquainted with evil.

'Of course, even if you did say something,' she added, 'no one would believe you.'

'I . . . I . . . ' I couldn't speak.

'Don't try,' she said. 'I warn you. Believe me. Don't try.'

Without another word, I left the parlour.

* * *

I'm going to leave Shadow Valley first thing tomorrow morning. I will not return this summer for a vacation on the old homestead. Nor shall I ever return.

Nor shall I ever marry. I don't intend to take any chances.

One of my children might be a girl, young and slender and bright and beautiful.

And something . . . *final* . . . might happen to me and to my wife, and our child would leave our home to live with her only living relative.

In Shadow Valley. With Cousin Anna.

I wouldn't want my daughter to see on her table what I saw on Anna's when I left.

A brand-new box of chocolates, wrapped in an old-fashioned box that was already coated with a thin layer of dust but was still gaudy with satin and ribbons.

It sat open on a table in the parlour. With one piece missing.

24

Two lines down from the final words, there had been a date: June 24th followed by a year now nearly three decades past.

The next page was blank.

Lila gently laid the journal down on the couch and, after a few moments' thought, left Mattie's parlour and returned to the upstairs room, the first one by the stairs.

I've read the journal . . . for all the good it's done. Now it's up to you, Rachel. Do your part.

The door stood open, the light was on. The Bible on the reading desk was open, just as it had been when Lila had walked into the room the last time. Most of the pages were flipped to the front, leaving only those few at the back, including the ones with the information on Obadiah Stevenson and wives number two, three, and four.

This time, Lila was sure she would see

another name linked to Obadiah's at the top of the page.

She did.

Obadiah Stevenson had married (first) Mattie Tresham.

But unlike the three other pages Lila had been permitted to read in the sealed book, this one — ornamented as profusely as had been the others — was packed with rows of tiny print, names of husbands and wives, linked to children by equally tiny lines.

She scanned the page quickly, looking for . . .

That had to be the one.

Mattie's youngest girl, Susannah, had married a man named Curtis Griff, and a small notation beside the entry indicated that the couple had married in, and remained to live in, Shadow Valley. Many of the rest of the notations named a different town, Oak Park. That was the place mentioned in the journal where Mattie had moved following Great-granddad's death, where she and her children had remained, while Rachel and Annie stayed there in Shadow Park.

'None of Mattie's kids came back to Shadow Valley except Grandma, when she got married.'

The journalist's grandmother had been Susannah Griff.

Curtis and Susannah Griff had given birth to a girl named Marie. She had married someone from out of state, a man named Russell Chatterton. Their only child was born far from Shadow Valley, and Marie had died giving birth to him. His name was Marshall Chatterton.

Marshall Chatterton.

The intrepid journalist. Tracked down at last.

Lila felt a rush of satisfaction. Although the page gave no further information about the Chattertons, she could at least put a name to the journalist, could begin constructing some sort of image of him that would allow for the wildness of his tale and his eccentric perspectives on so many of his relatives. Including Aunt Annie, his half-great-aunt.

That thought sent Lila back to the page and in only a few seconds she had found another name she needed.

There it was. One of Susannah's other children, another daughter named Mae. She had married Walton Jay of Oak Park. They had had a single child, also a daughter, named Anna Elizabeth. Mae had also died in childbirth.

Cousin Anna.

Lila was beginning to see patterns forming in the family lines. Terrible, almost horrifying patterns. Couples bearing only one or two children, usually daughters. Mothers dying in childbirth. Motherless children left to be raised by grieving widowers or husbandless grandmothers.

Lila checked one more time.

Yes, another small notation beside Anna Jay's name indicated that after the death of her Grandmother Susannah, she had been taken in by a nephew of Curtis Jay . . . Evan Jay and his wife Vera.

Of Shadow Valley.

And the circle was complete.

Lila felt as if she knew everyone now. She mentally constructed charts filled with names, drawing imaginary arrows from one to another, until the intricate web of relationships was completed. And through them all, the three women: Rachel, Annie, and Anna.

Anna Elizabeth.

Almost as an afterthought, Lila found herself wondering what kinds of nicknames the mid-twentieth century would have had for *Elizabeth*. *Liz*, to be sure. And *Lizzy* — an awful name to call anyone, Lila decided, but especially an energetic and beautiful young woman. *Bett. Betty. Beth.*

What about . . . *Ella?*

Lila went cold.

'*You may call me Ella.*'

Lila suddenly flashed on being a senior in high school. Their English teacher, a squat toad of a woman named Mrs. Schraver, had begun one day by handing out copies of a thick book, so thick that Lila had half-believed that it had to contain not one but a hundred novels. Without being told to, she immediately opened it to the first page and read the first line.

That was her standard practice with any book. If the first line didn't capture her attention, she would slip the book back onto the shelf and quietly forget about it. Of course, she would *have* to read this one, regardless of the first line. Either read it or flunk twelfth-grade English.

She still remembered the line, in part because it was so short — although it was, in fact, the entire first paragraph — and in part because it raised a question that, to her intense dissatisfaction, had never been answered, not even after hundreds of pages of dense text.

'Call me Ishmael.'

Not 'My name is Ishmael.' *Call me Ishmael*.

'*You may call me Ella.*'

'Ella?' Lila spoke the name out loud for the first time in some while, but this time she felt as if there were a good chance she would be answered. 'Ella? Anna? Anna Elizabeth?'

Nothing.

She was ready to leave the room, certain that she had gleaned every last bit of information from the Bible that was possible . . . or at least necessary, when her eye happened upon another name.

Her world went black. For a moment she thought she had passed out . . . or rather, wished that she had passed out and was now waking up and that this whole wretched string of events had been part of some horrific nightmare, yet another result of 'undigested bit of beef, a blot of mustard, a crumb of cheese, a fragment of an underdone potato,' even though she had eaten nothing for hours.

That was it! She hadn't eaten since that miserable sandwich at noon, and she was hungry and her mind was playing tricks on her, sending her hallucinations that would simply become more and more appalling, more obscene, until she roused herself, went out to her car, and dug out another sandwich from the cooler. That was all that was wrong. She simply needed food.

She knew that was not the case, however.

The evidence was there, scribbled in faded black ink, a list of names running down the far edge of the page, some of the letters half-obscured by the decorative border. Most of them, however, were legible.

Obadiah Stevenson had married Mattie Tresham.

Nothing new there, but the familiarity did nothing to calm Lila.

Their eldest daughter, Delilah Stevenson, had married Matthew Brandon.

That union was blessed with four children, only one of which survived the great influenza epidemic of 1918, when hundreds of thousands of people lost their lives in a matter of weeks.

The surviving child was — *what else?* — a daughter. Annelisa Brandon.

Nothing to worry about there, just another detail in a pattern.

Except that Annelisa was Lila's own grandmother's name.

Annelisa had married Elden Janssen, who, another notation stated, had deserted her before their only child was born: Lisa Anne Janssen.

The record was complete.

In a scrawl pressed into the remaining bit of white space at the bottom of the page, someone had reported the marriage of Lisa Anne Janssen to Cornelius Ellis. And thus Lisa Anne Janssen became Lisa Anne Ellis. Lila's mother.

She found her own name among the whirls and swirls of foliage: *Lila Anne Ellis*. Unmarried.

This time she actually did faint.

25

When Lila regained consciousness, she was resting on the couch in Mattie's parlor. She had no idea how she had gotten there, whether she had made her way in the midst of some somnambulistic trance, or whether she had been spirited there by a power or powers unseen. Nor did she particularly care.

Her mind was too full of what she had read and with its implications for her to wonder more than a moment.

Then she sat up and looked for the journal.

It was on the end table.

She grabbed it and began frantically turning pages, looking for one specific line. She knew that it was in the last part, close to the end.

Desperately she thumbed through the pages, scanning bits and pieces until her eyes settled on what she knew was there. Marshall — what a relief it was to have a name for the writer — had been visiting Anna, sitting with her in this very room. She had made a peculiar statement: 'We're the last, aren't we. The last of Rachel's line.'

Lila hadn't thought much about it when she had first read it. Her knowledge of the intricate genealogical ties in the Stevenson line had been vague at best. The words had more or less rolled over her.

Then Marshall had begun saying something: "'No,' I said. 'We're not even related to Rachel. She was only Grandma's . . .'"

Anna had not let him finish his statement.

Lila could do so now, with the full authority of the Bible entries. Rachel had been Susannah Stevenson Griff's aunt by marriage only. There were no blood ties between Rachel — and Annie — and either Marshall or his cousin Anna Elizabeth Jay, his cousin Anna.

Yet that had made no difference to Anna during her conversation with Marshall. She considered herself 'of Rachel's line.'

How . . . and why?

A dreadful thought surfaced in Lila's mind.

Cousin Anna had been *herself* when she entered Rachel's parlor that final night. Then *something* had happened, and from the next morning on, she was someone *different*.

She behaved differently. She looked differently. She spoke differently. She had already begun to put on weight, just as Aunt Annie had immediately following Rachel's death . . . after she had been alone with Rachel's burnt corpse in the kitchen of the old house . . . again, Lila reminded herself, *this house*.

Even if the bizarre account of some kaleidoscopic whirlwind of women was patently impossible, *something* had happened. Each time, a bright, beautiful, intelligent young woman had become almost an appendage of Rachel.

As if Rachel had in some way taken over the other person.

As if her own daughter . . . and then decades later, the great-granddaughter of her bitterest enemy had become . . . what, little more than *cattle* to Rachel.

Bodies to infest. And then to corrupt.

It was impossible, of course.

But *if* . . .

We're the last, aren't we. The last of Rachel's line.

But that wasn't true. The Bible upstairs proved that. There was at least one other person, descended mother to daughter from Mattie Tresham Stevenson, now sitting on the sofa in Mattie's parlor.

Herself.

Lila bit back a scream. Intellectually, she knew that everything she was thinking was impossible, a nightmare. But emotionally, deep within, where her rational functions were being held prisoner by her rampaging emotions, she *believed*.

Come one, come all! Seeing is Believing! And Believing is . . .

She was next.

Or perhaps not.

The journal had ended abruptly, with Russell Chatterton's stated intentions never to return to Shadow Valley and never to marry . . . never to run the risk of fathering a daughter to continue the tainted line.

But maybe Russell had married after all. Maybe he did have a daughter. Maybe he had become the father to a clutch of daughters, each of them making her way to Shadow Valley at that very instant, drawn by the ineluctable strands of maternity, ancestry, and destiny. Maybe the line was not dead.

Lila began turning the blank pages of the journal. It was possible, wasn't it, that Marshall had continued his story later, after he had left Shadow Valley . . .

But then how did his journal end up in the house? Why was it lying on that shelf, by itself, just waiting for her to pick it up and begin reading.

Page after page flipped past.

Nothing.

Not a single blot of ink. Not a single line, not a word.

Until Lila flipped the last page over and saw what had been pasted onto the flyleaf at the end of the journal.

It was a newspaper clipping, neatly cut from a larger page. It had already turned that distinctive yellow-brown that old newsprint takes on, and Lila knew that if she tried to lift it from the flyleaf, no matter how carefully and no matter how old and fragile the paste had become, the paper would simply disintegrate.

It even *smelled* old.

She began reading.

The body of Marshall Chatterton — it said — had been discovered the day before in the driver's seat of his overturned car just beyond where the highway divided at Point of the Mountain. He had probably been returning from a visit in Shadow Valley to his home — he was a native and life-long resident of Los Angeles — when his car had veered off the two-lane road and upended in an irrigation ditch. There had been no water in the ditch at the time.

The investigating officers were not clear as to the cause of the incident. There were no obstructions in the roadway, no tracks or skid marks to indicate that the deceased had jammed on his brakes and slid out of control. No witnesses had been found to what had occurred, and no trace of a second vehicle was discovered.

Tests had subsequently showed no drugs or alcohol in the deceased's blood.

Cause of death was readily apparent, however. Somehow, as the vehicle had rolled, Marshall Chatterton had been thrust up against the floor-mounted gearshift, which — for reasons unknown to anyone who had spoken with him during his one-day stay in Shadow Valley — did not have a shift knob.

The shift lever, unusually long and thin and surmounted by sharp steel threads, had pierced his chest, shattering the manubrium of his sternum and then continuing — almost as if it had been thrust with inhuman strength — through his thoracic cavity, slashing his heart and fracturing his ribcage as it exited along his spine.

The county coroner was at a loss to explain the precise mechanism of death — why the lever had penetrated so far. He had hesitated to use words like *impale* and *gore* but admitted that in his forty years of service with the Coroner's Office he had never seen a wound even

260

remotely similar.

Someone should have warned Mr. Chatterton, he concluded, of the dangers of driving with exposed threads on the shifting lever.

Lila rather thought that someone had. And she knew who it must have been.

The report of Chatterton's death was awful enough — he was, as she now knew, in some technical manner cousins . . . second cousins, probably, with a removal or two added in for good measure. And she had come to know him in an odd way as she had read his words.

The truly horrifying part of his death, however, was not revealed until Lila sat back and, almost in shock from imagining the details of his death, allowed her eyes to drift to the top of the article. There was the requisite compressed, impersonal headline: 'Shadow Valley Visitor Dead in Auto Accident.'

But above that, separated by a thin black line that had almost faded away, and set in such small type that she had great difficulty reading it, was one more bit of information.

The date that the newspaper was printed.

June 26.

The day after he had written the final lines in his journal and dated them. The day he intended to leave Shadow Valley, never to return again.

There was no subsequent marriage, no daughters.

And Lila *was* the last of the line.

26

Her first thought was to escape. To get out of the house. *Now!*

She raced to the front door.

She had to have a breath of fresh air or she would suffocate. She had to be away from the underlying taint of chocolate and dust and age and death that was everywhere in the house. She had to *leave*, no matter the time of night or day when she got out. She would try to start her car. And if that failed, she would *walk* — she would follow the drive back down to the road and from there make her way back to Main Street and follow it up the rise until she was in the shadow of the single remaining wall of the old church.

Surely she would be safe there.

If she was careful, she could walk — make that *run* — down the middle of the worn roads, avoiding the rose canes with their scythe-like thorns.

Considering what she had learned in

this house, rose bushes were the least of her worries.

Except that the front door was locked.

Not just locked, but immobile.

She knew what that meant.

Whatever was going on in the house was not over. There were after all, two more rooms — excepting the kitchen, which she intuitively felt might be a kind of neutral ground, claimed by neither Rachel nor Mattie — two more rooms that she had not yet been allowed to enter.

The front corner bedroom directly above Rachel's parlour.

And Rachel's parlour itself.

She tried the pocket doors first, with little hope that they would open. Her heart told her that she would have to make one final trip up the stairs and along the dark hallway to the room where Rachel and Annie had slept ... to Rachel's room. Lila had already been in Annie's and found nothing terrifying there. In fact, given the apparitions that had haunted the remaining bedrooms, the old-fashioned bed and the treadle sewing machine now seemed normal and conventional.

No, it would be Rachel's bedroom, the room she originally shared with Obadiah Stevenson and then allowed only her daughter to enter.

Resignedly, Lila turned away from the front door and made her way to the stairs.

As she did so, the light in Mattie's parlour went out, followed a second later by the light in the lower hall itself. Only reflected light from the second floor remained, but it was enough for her to climb the stairs toward whatever awaited.

And something, she knew, surely awaited.

At the top of the stairs, she took a moment to look down the hall.

All of the doors were closed. No hint of light escaped, either from keyholes bored into worn brass facing plates, or from thin cracks along top, bottom, and side to indicate that the doors might be ajar and that lights were glowing within.

And everything was silent.

The house had been preternaturally silent all night, with none of the expected *creaks* and *cracks* of an old wooden place settling on its foundations. There had been no furtive scrabbling of vermin in corners or on shelves or in cabinets. The only sounds had been those the house *wanted* Lila to hear, summoning her to another unwelcome revelation leading to the final truth.

That she was the real victim here.

But now, the silence hung even more heavily. It was as if nothing *could* be heard, even if a book had abruptly fallen from its place on the book case shelf, or one of the sconces had slipped its moorings and plummeted through shadowed depths before crashing on the floor. Even if there had been a sound, it would not have carried through the dense, oppressive air.

Lila felt as if her ears had been plugged, restricting all hearing to the pounding her own heart and the rapid pulsing of her own blood.

She didn't even bother to try the intervening doors. She walked directly to the corner front bedroom and rested her fingers on the knob.

It was *cold*. Icy cold.

She drew back. The knob had felt so frigid that at first she was afraid that she had left bits of flesh adhering to it, like a child who touches a damp tongue to a metal flagpole on the coldest day of the year and then finds it impossible to back away without great pain and suffering. She glanced down at her fingertips. They appeared whole and unharmed.

She did not try to open the door again, not yet.

Instead she brought her ear close to the wooden panel, not quite touching it but very nearly so.

She shut her eyes, concentrating all of her senses on hearing.

Yes, there was something. A faint hum. Not a rise and swell of static, like what one would hear by placing one's ear next to a conch shell ... that almost hackneyed and too, too commonplace echo of one's own heart and blood.

No, this was something different. This was a nearly inaudible susurrus — a whisper, a murmur of myriad voices, none loud enough to be heard over the attempts of the others, none conspicuous enough to allow her to understand what words might underlie the sounds. She felt that if she could only come nearer, even an inch or two, if she could only focus infinitesimally more on the sounds, she would understand . . . *everything*, not just the words they were whispering but the secrets behind the words, the darkness behind the secrets, and the infinite emptiness behind the darkness.

She felt almost *compelled* to move closer.

Some remaining voice of reason countered the compulsion.

Instead, she drew away.

There was something in the room, of that she was certain. Someone, perhaps, but certainly *something*. More than anything, she wanted — *needed* — to know who or what it was . . . and she feared finding out with all her being. Even away from the door, she could still hear the sound, as if the act of concentrating had linked her to it, made it inevitable that she and whoever — whatever — was speaking would meet.

And that she would be forever altered.

She almost retreated.

Surely if she made her way down the stairs, she could find a way out of the house. The front door might still be locked, inviolable. But there were the windows in the parlour. Mattie's parlour. One had broken earlier that day. Perhaps she would be able to throw something — the books from the case — through the panes, break enough of them that she could then force her way through the frame and out onto the porch and from there escape the house and its shadows and its secrets and its . . . its whispering.

If the doors to Mattie's parlour are unlocked and open, reason whispered.

They might be, Lila thought frantically. They had been all night. There was no justification for simply assuming that they would be locked. She could still turn around, make her way down the stairs and, even if the ground-floor hall was in darkness, feel her way along the wall and into the parlour. She had been there often enough that she knew she could find the drapes hanging in front of the windows, pull them open, shatter a window, and . . .

She turned the doorknob.

It was still cold, but this time, as if listening to the *hummm* had inoculated her against its worst effects, it was not so bitter. Her fingers felt chilled but not numbed, not damaged.

She turned the knob, felt the mechanism disengage and the door begin to swing free.

The door to Rachel's sanctuary.

Almost without breathing, she pushed, feeling the doorway open to reveal . . .

Nothing.

Literally nothing.

It was not that the room was without furniture, or that there were no bleeding bodies strewn around as if in the aftermath of some hideous accident, or even that there was nothing but ancient, peeling newsprint on the walls.

There was nothing *behind the door.*

Solid, featureless, blank *nothingness.*

It was not even darkness or blackness.

Instead, she felt — to the deepest marrow of her bones — an *absence* that stunned her beyond anything she could have imagined.

Almost giddily, she recalled a popular schoolyard riddle from when she was a child.

Can nothing *be* something?

She and her friends had argued the abstract philosophical point around and around without ever understanding that it was abstract or philosophical. For them, it was simply a game with words. It meant nothing. The debate accomplished nothing.

But now she knew that, if asked that question again — can *nothing* be *something?* — she would have the answer.

Yes, because this room contains *nothing.*

She had no idea whether there were walls inside the room, or whether the emptiness within extended from her to the farthest reaches of the farthest galaxy. It felt in her heart as if it might.

And there was the *hummm,* louder now that the door was open but still so attenuated that she could easily have convinced herself that she heard nothing at all. Except that she knew better.

She took a small step toward the door jamb. Even this close, she could see . . . nothing.

She reached out her finger, moving it with infinite care lest she actually *touch* the boundary between her world and . . . whatever was before her.

Then, holding her breath as if she were about to plunge from the highest platform and plummet into water deeper than any she had ever known, she touched the emptiness.

Nothing.

No force holding her back, no pressure pulling at her to suck her into the darkness.

She let her hand move an inch or so further in.

It looked as if some master surgeon had amputated her fingers at the first joint, so adroitly that nothing remained to suggest that the tips had ever existed. Her skin stretched smoothly across her knuckles, her too, too solid flesh and blood visible beneath the thin covering.

And then it stopped.

She felt no pain. She didn't even feel as if the tips of her fingertips had disappeared. They were not cold, were not numb, and if she wriggled them — she knew that she was doing so, because she could see movement in the tissue that was visible — she felt them move. It was as if . . .

Something touched her.

She screamed but did not move. She could not move.

The susurrus increased, not in loudness but in intensity. It was as if a message had been sent and received that something . . . *physical* . . . had intruded. Throughout the universe of nothingness, the word had been spread.

Again, the feather-light touch. And another. And another.

One more, Lila felt, and they would grasp her fingers, weave themselves into an unstoppable force, and yank her into . . .

She ran.

She didn't look back, she simply ran down the hallway and clattered — *oh blessed sound oh joyous noise* — down the stairs.

27

She reached the bottom without tripping on her own feet and falling.

As she stepped onto the hallway floor, the light upstairs winked out and the one nearer the front door flickered on. She began to move forward, intending first to try the front door to see if it was locked; and then, if it was, to try the doors to Mattie's Parlour.

She never had the chance.

'Lila, dear.'

She slowly turned.

At the top of the stairway stood a tall figure wearing a long white gown, its hem rippling as if in a slight breeze. She recognized the face.

'Ella,' Lila said.

The figure nodded.

'Or is it Anna? Or Annie?'

Another mute nod.

'Or are you Rachel? Or none of them? Or all of them?

The woman waved one hand negligently as if to say, *your choice, my dear, so you must choose. I am satisfied with any*.

'Rachel, then. Because I believe that is who you *really* are.'

The figure did not respond, either to Lila's words or to the tone of her voice.

'What is it you want? What was that . . . that *nothingness* upstairs? Are you going to show me something more now, something to paralyze me with fright?'

The figure took one step forward and began descending the stairway, so slowly that it seemed as if a dozen breaths must pass between each step. Step, pause. Step, pause. Step, pause.

It looked like some monstrous parody of a wedding march, blushing bride in virginal white step-step-stepping down the stairs in time with the music being pumped out by an ancient organ. Step-step-step.

Although this bride was not blushing but pale as death. And Lila doubted if anyone could think of the thing approaching her as virginal. Perhaps it had never

known the joys of human sexual inter-
course, but it was anything but pure and
untouched.

Lila backed down the hall, toward the
front door.

Even as she did so, though, she
struggled to keep her eyes fixed on the
figure descending the stairway. It was
difficult to do so. It hurt — it physically
hurt to watch the figure as it grew closer.
On one step, it was clearly Rachel, already
familiar from the lithograph hanging
— *where is it* hanging *now?* — that had
transformed her into a harridan, this
Rachel aged by decades, her hair
straggling around her face, hand gnarled
and arthritic, fingers curled into claws,
her eyes pinioning Lila. On the next
tread, it was someone else entirely,
although the resemblance to Rachel's
portrait was clear — this woman was
larger, grossly obese, swathed neck to foot
in a nineteenth-century gown that seemed
to have burned at the sleeves. On the
next, a conflation of the two that swirled
and intertwined until Lila's head began to
ache. It felt as if her eyes were being

pulled two, three, a hundred different directions at once, each eye moving separately from the other until she was sure her skull would simply fragment.

Another step, and it was yet a different woman — a not-Rachel, not-Annie, not-Anna that was still in some terrible way the essence of all three simultaneously

Another step, and it was even more . . . different. A core of something dark and empty around which coiled RachelAnnaAnnie, each flashing in an out of existence in a heartbeat only to recur another heartbeat later.

And so it went, step by step.

Step-step-step.

When the figure — Ella for certain this time . . . or was it? — placed her foot on the hall floor, Lila had backed all of the way to the front door. With her right hand behind her, she was struggling to release the lock that had turned so easily for her earlier that night.

Only now it stuck. She could feel her fingers slipping on the knob, damp with sweat and fear, but the latch would not turn.

The smell of chocolate — which she had almost ceased to notice long before — suddenly grew stronger.

Ella — or was it Anna now, or Annie, the figure shifted so rapidly that Lisa's eyes burned — approached. Her goal was not Lila, however, as she pressed her back against her only escape, but the sealed pocket doors on the wall opposite the parlour. As the figure drew closer, something inside the doors snapped, a violent, vicious, wrenching sound that contained within it all of the agonies of the lost in Hell, and the heavy wooden panels began to separate, disappearing inch by inch into the wall on each side.

Revealing, at last, the hidden room. Rachel's parlour.

At the threshold, the figure halted. With one hand, it gestured toward Lila, and then toward the room.

Enter, my dear, enter and be relieved of worry, of care, of loneliness, of the thousand griefs and torments of each long and wearisome day.

Lila moved, not so much toward the opening as to circle it. As she did so, the room gradually came into view, brilliantly lit by a crystal chandelier that put the paltry fixture in Mattie's parlour to shame.

The room was rich, luxuriant, ornamented in high-Victorian mode with heavy dark mahogany furniture that glistened beneath the lights. A huge oval table stood in the centre . . . although curiously enough, there were no matching chairs. That was actually to the good, since the top of the table was heaped with boxes of every shape . . . square, rectangle, oblong, oval, heart-shaped. In the brilliance, the boxes shimmered with satin, velvet, with slick enamel-like finishes, with softer moire, with silk so fine that it seemed an endless sheen. There were ribbons of every imaginable variety, of a score of fabrics, each capturing, holding, then violently casting back the light. And all in an infinite variety of red and scarlet and crimson and cardinal, as fresh as if each had just left the hand of the storekeeper.

The scent of chocolate was overpowering.

Beyond the table lay a maze of furniture . . . furniture, furniture, and more furniture. An armchair upholstered in plush Dobonnet, the colour so vibrant that for an instant Lila thought she smelled . . . no, *tasted* herbs and raisin at the back of her tongue. A waist-high bow-front cabinet polished to an almost metallic gleam held more boxes, innumerable boxes as scintillating as those on the table. A reed organ — deep blood-toned cherry-wood this time, its nine-foot height carved into niches and small shelves faced with bevelled mirrors. Its keys were ebony and polished ivory, and the velvet facing its sounding box was the red of arterial blood.

There was more, more than Lila could take in: end tables and deal tables and footstools and Inglenook chairs on either side of the fireplace and a couch before the drape-shrouded window and a glass-fronted display cabinet filled with photographs in silver frames . . . except that Lila could not quite see *who* might be in the photographs. The images faded in and out so rapidly that the kaleidoscopic effect made her dizzy.

Above the fireplace hung a framed lithograph of a rather severe-looking woman wearing a high-necked, formal-looking gown in the style of the late nineteenth-century. At her neck was a narrow fringe of lace. Her eyes -- irises pale against the deep darkness of the pupils — seemed to survey the room with intense satisfaction.

Along the far wall was a highboy — the same highboy that Marshall had described in his journal, she was certain — piled high with yet more boxes, some tightly closed, some open to reveal small mounds of chocolate and . . .

And legions of mice, mostly hidden in the stark shadows cast by the chandelier but some darting out to nibble and paw and scrape at the candies.

Lila felt a sudden revulsion that began in the pit of her stomach and flooded outward, a tidal wave that engulfed her just long enough for the light to dim, the glitter to become tawdry and cheap, the furniture to reveal its decades-long covering of dust and droppings, the colors to fade to dingy and drab and leaden.

She started back.

The figure moved her arm in a gesture of invitation . . . and the richness returned, doubled and tripled.

Enter, my dear, enter and be relieved of worry, of care, of loneliness, of the thousand griefs and torments of each long and wearisome day.

Enter, my dear, and all will be yours to enjoy, a timeless time of pleasure and sweetness and richness and luxury.

The woman — Ella again, solid and opaque and still — held a single piece of chocolate in her hand. She smiled and extended it toward Lila.

28

An observer standing on a sage-mottled ridge overlooking an old, ramshackle farmhouse at the moment of dawn, looking down into a long-neglected yard containing hillocks of weeds, the remnants of farm equipment long-since rusted into disuse, and — something quite out of place with the rest of the landscape — a late-model car parked a dozen feet from the porch, would have seen a sight at once both curious and commonplace.

With a bone-rattling *thump* the front door to the old place abruptly opened, thrown back with such force that it must have smashed against the inner wall. The sound echoed across the swale, bouncing from ridge to ridge. Several half-awakened birds took flight, arcing away from the farmstead to disappear into the west.

The jarring interruption into the peace of a late-summer morning faded, followed by several long minutes of absolute silence. Not an insect *chirrup*-ed, not a breath of breeze rustled the leaves of the trees overhanging the house.

Then a young woman appeared on the porch. She stood there for a long while, staring into the open yard and seeming to do little more than breathe — deeply and, to all appearances, with great relish, as if the morning air tasted unusually sweet.

She stepped out of the shadows, down the three dilapidated steps, and onto the hard-packed earth that served as a walkway leading up to the house. Just short of the car, she stopped, drew a cell phone from her pocket, stared at it for a moment, then punched in a series of numbers. She must have reached whomever she was calling, because she spoke a few words, nodding as she did so, and then broke the connection.

After a pause in which she did nothing except stare into an unseen distance, she turned, ascended the three steps, and disappeared into the shadows.

The preternatural silence continued unbroken. It was as if every living thing within earshot was waiting ... for something as yet unknown.

When she reappeared, the young woman was carrying a single object. Although covered with a bit of worn fabric, its shape and dimensions suggested a large picture frame. She walked around the car and opened the back door on the passenger side. It took a bit of maneuvering, but she managed to slide the frame into the back seat, propping it against the upholstery.

When she apparently was satisfied that the frame would not slip, she stepped back, shut the door quietly, as if not to break the surrounding silence, and disappeared back into the house.

The delay was longer this time.

When she emerged, she was carrying another object. This one was more difficult to identify. It was smaller, oblong, a box of some sort covered with nondescript wrapping that from a distance looked washed out, as if it had once been red but had long since faded to nearly grey. This she placed on the back seat next to the frame.

Closing the car door with a finality that

clearly indicated that she had nothing more to place on the back seat, she stood for a while longer, looking around slowly as if she were trying to imprint every detail of the landscape onto her memory. She stared for a long time at the house itself, barely blinking the whole time.

Then shaking her head as if to bring herself back to the here and the now, she walked around the car, opened the driver's door, and slid in.

A moment later the car started, its engine purring smoothly, the only sound in the pervasive silence.

She maneuvered the car around until it was facing down the pitted, clogged driveway, and then with infinite care, piloted it away from the house and toward the distant hedgerow dotted with the remnants of overblown wild roses. When she turned to the left, apparently heading back toward what remained of Shadow Valley, the sound of the engine faded almost as soon as the car itself disappeared from sight.

Behind her, the farmyard remained silent, nothing moving.

29

A week after Lila Ellis delivered the final quit-claim form to her supervisor on the Shadow Valley Reservoir project, officially declaring that all of the properties within the designated area legally belonged — part and parcel — to the state, unnamed employees depressed the appropriate buttons and pulled the appropriate levers to close emergency spillways, and the water that had once tumbled from the valley in a handful of creeks and streams began to back up behind the newly completed dams.

At first, there was little change to the valley. The late summer sun baked the gravel roadways as usual, causing shimmering heat waves to distort the air. Milkweeds along the fences flaunted their wonted dusty grey-green foliage and began to open their pods to release flights of silky floss into the sky. Second-crop raspberries ripened on their canes, although no one was around to pick the plump, sweet fruit. Now and then a solitary coyote might nose around the remains of a chicken coop, drawn by the lingering scent long after the succulent birds had been removed.

But gradually, as with all things of the world, the landscape altered. First the smaller creeks overflowed their banks, almost as if there had been a typical early-spring thaw on Mount Cleveland, except this time the waters did not finally withdraw back to their normal banks. Instead, they continued to rise, to spread dark fingers into shadowy corners where they had never before intruded. And with each passing day, each passing hour, the water consumed more and more of the valley.

What had once been Myrtle Hodgfield's treasured truck garden drowned quickly, located as it had been near the edge of one of the valley's larger streams. The water flowed over the ground she had once so patiently kept free of weeds, and spread across the level beds in a matter of minutes.

It lapped curiously at the base of shattered brickwork that marked the remnants of Gilda and Elihu Pettingale's once notoriously noxious fireplace, although the scent of *Eau de raccoon* had long before disappeared.

It invaded the foundations of Evan and Vera Ellsworth's home, first filling the remains of the basement, then trailing along the path leading to the site of collapsed barns and outbuildings.

It crawled up the rise at the north end of Main Street, inch by inch, until it spilled over into the ruins of the old chapel, finally covering the lone remaining wall that had, long before sheltered Lila Ellis as she napped.

Bit by bit it engulfed whatever signs still lingered of generations of love and loss, the water — nature's universal solvent — first burying, then beginning its insidious work of softening and altering and dissolving and finally leaving the detritus lying undisturbed deep beneath the surface.

30

Mable Sykes was ninety-six years young and proud of every year. She kept her own home — a nice little two-bedroom clapboard on a nice little street cluttered with other old houses. She did her own washing and ironing, her own cooking and cleaning. She had a rigid schedule, which was what she claimed kept her going all these years, and she followed it punctiliously.

Right now, she looked up at the grandmother clock on her mantle.

It was right on time, down to the minute, down to the old second hand stuttering its way across the cracked enamel face. She had received that clock as a wedding gift when she married the late Mr. Sykes, now nearly forty years in his grave, and she would smugly reassure visitors, when she had some, that it had never lost a minute in all those years . . . as long as she remembered to wind it once a week. Of course, with her carefully observed schedule, she never forgot.

In a way, the clock had become a redundancy, since her own internal clock — and the television that ran nearly twenty-four hours each day because of her insomnia — kept her well informed of the minute and hour.

And all three told her that it was time to get up from her La-Z-boy, a gift from her third grandson on her eighty-fifth, turn down the sound on her afternoon shows, and get herself settled by the window for what over the years had become her favourite daytime occupation.

Neighbourhood Watch.

Not that she was part of any organized programme established by the others living on her street to serve and protect in whatever small way she could.

No, indeed.

She *watched* the *neighbours!*

In the long run, that was far more interesting than any of the soaps she had followed now for nearly five decades.

And for the past several months, there had been a new character in her

Neighbourhood Watch. Just around Thanksgiving last year, a sweet young thing had moved into the empty house right across the way from Mabel's own place. At first, Mabel thought that perhaps the young woman would soon be followed by a husband, but no young man ever materialized. For the first few weeks, the woman had busied herself around the house, eradicating the few weeds that had encroached onto the lawn while the place had been empty, trimming the rose bushes that formed a thick hedge between her yard and the neighbors on either side, cutting back the wayward branches of the old apricot in the middle of the lawn, the one whose branches would be budding and blooming in a month or so.

Then gradually, the young woman had stopped.

Now, part of the excitement of Mabel's Neighbourhood Watch included wondering whether she would catch sight of the young woman or not. She had become like an elusive warbler or a rare woodpecker to an avid birdwatcher . . . not something to capture or kill, just something to note as having been *seen*.

She hadn't been seen at all for the past week. Mabel had begun to worry about the poor thing. About whether she might be sick, although that was not a first-rank worry, since lights went on and off regularly, curtains occasionally shifted in the three windows Mabel could see, mail disappeared from the black enamel mailbox next to the front door, although Mabel never actually *saw* the young woman step outside to collect it ... it mostly looked like junk, anyway, circulars from the local stores, offers for AOL link-ups, advertisements from nearby chiropractors and dentists — the sorts of things Mabel found in her own box.

She worried about whether the young woman might be lonely. Mabel had been lonely for many long years herself, before her schedule had developed sufficient complexity to keep her mind off it, so she understood how the young woman might be feeling.

Not that Mabel herself would ever be able to make it across the street and visit her, not at *ninety-six*, but she decided that the young woman might legitimately be pining for visitors her own age.

No one ever came to the house across the street. And Mabel watched carefully, even when she was not seated in front of her window, in her favourite chair, with her binoculars — a gift from her second grandson on her ninetieth.

No one came to the house across the street. No young men looking eager to see their lady-love after an entire day's separation. No friends come to chat about this and that and share favorite recipes. Not even any cable repairmen — was the cable even working in that house? — or termite inspectors or kids peddling the local newspaper.

Day after day, hour after hour, the door remained steadfastly closed, as if it had been securely locked and the young woman had lost her only key.

Except, of course, that no locksmith ever came.

Mabel glanced both ways down the street.

It was that time of afternoon. Children had finished their homework and might receive permission from harried mothers to play in the front yard — not that there were that many children on the block, but even one or two playing hop-scotch or catch made for a nice break. Sometimes they even smiled and waved at Mabel.

Fathers would be coming home from work soon, crawling down the street at exactly the speed limit, turning tiredly into well-worn driveways and disappearing into attached garages, to reappear perhaps fifteen minutes, perhaps half an hour later to putter around the yard, snipping and clipping in the cool winter evenings until wives called out that dinner was ready.

Sometimes . . . wait, now that's something new.

A delivery truck was making its way slowly down the street, pausing here and there as if the driver were unfamiliar with the area and had to stop to check the address. Mabel decided to guess which house the truck would stop at. She had just decided on the faded pink two-story three houses down when . . .

Good lord, it was pulling up outside

the young woman's place.

Mabel sat up straight and pressed the binoculars so tightly against her eyes that her cheekbones began to ache.

Yes, he was getting out, going up the walkway, knocking on the door. Oh, but this was getting exciting. Mabel could feel her heart kick up a beat or two.

He was carrying something, but unfortunately he held it front of himself, so she couldn't quite see what it was.

Now he is knocking. Once. Twice. Three times. He pauses. One more knock.

Come on, come on, Mabel urged, *answer the door. He's not going to stand out there forever, you know.*

As if the young woman had heard her, the door opened.

Mabel straightened even further. If she hadn't been quite so excited, she would have noted that her spine was sending messages of outrage to her brain, but even if she had noted, she might not have cared.

Step outside, step outside, step outside.
And — all glory hallelujah — the young

woman did . . . or at least she opened the door enough that Mabel could see her quite clearly.

A sighting! A sighting!

The delivery man held out a clipboard for the young woman to sign. She took it and scribbled something, smiled as if she had been expecting this delivery for her whole life, and handed the clipboard back.

The delivery man slid it under his arm and, with his other hand, extended something out toward the young woman.

The money shot, Mabel thought, echoing a phrase she had heard on one of her programmes and blissfully unaware of some of its less savoury applications. She adjusted her binoculars and carefully focused on the package.

Ahh. Now that is interesting. Perhaps I won't be worrying about the sweet young thing being lonely for much longer.

She dropped her binoculars, sat back, sighed, and for the first time became aware that she was in some discomfort. Nothing that captivating had happened on her street for some time. On the whole, she decided, it had been worth a few aches and pains.

The woman across the street handed something to the delivery man — a tip perhaps — who started back to his truck. The young woman disappeared into the blackness of the house. The door closed.

But Mabel was satisfied. She glanced over at the small desk where, once a month, as regularly as clockwork, she sat to pay her few bills and write notes to her grandchildren. One corner held a stand-up calendar. The bank where she had kept her money for nearly seven decades sent her one each year.

As well they should! Small enough recognition of my loyalty!

She smiled.

February 14th. Valentine's Day.

Not that that meant anything to Mabel at her age, but she knew well enough what kind of packages came by special delivery on that particular day.

I hope it was a pound of chocolates. That was always my favourite.

She settled into her chair and, rather

desultorily, continued her Neighbourhood Watch. After that, anything would be anticlimactic. But it was restful.

So restful that she drifted off.

When she roused, she was furious at herself.

She had just missed another arrival. She thought that she could see a taxi-cab turning at the far end of the street, but it was so far away that she couldn't be certain.

It had to have been a cab, though, since there was really no other way the man now standing at the end of the young woman's walk could have arrived.

As she watched, he made his way to the door. He seemed young, certainly younger than the delivery man had been, and he walked with a peculiarly jaunty step that Mabel found sweetly charming.

I'll bet I know why he is here, she thought the moment she realized that he was carrying a small bouquet of flowers.

This is even better than my soaps. She hummed quietly, a satisfied smile on her withered lips. She could not know that she had watched the last show she would ever watch only an hour before, and that before this evening ended, she would be embarking on an entirely new yet not entirely unanticipated adventure, one with herself in a starring role.

She went to rise, intending to return to her La-Z-boy and rest for a while. She didn't want to snoop any further on the young woman across the street and her new young man . . . plenty of time for that later.

'He must be with the state police,' she muttered as she began the short walk back to her recliner — a short walk she would never complete. 'Or maybe a forest ranger. Yes, that's it. A forest ranger, just coming off duty and so eager to see his new love that he doesn't even stop to change out of his uniform.'

She chuckled.

'I do wonder, though, why they keep on wearing those funny hats!'

THE END

We do hope that you have enjoyed reading this large print book.

Did you know that all of our titles are available for purchase?

We publish a wide range of high quality large print books including:

**Romances, Mysteries, Classics
General Fiction
Non Fiction and Westerns**

Special interest titles available in large print are:

**The Little Oxford Dictionary
Music Book, Song Book
Hymn Book, Service Book**

Also available from us courtesy of Oxford University Press:

**Young Readers' Dictionary
(large print edition)
Young Readers' Thesaurus
(large print edition)**

For further information or a free brochure, please contact us at:
**Ulverscroft Large Print Books Ltd.,
The Green, Bradgate Road, Anstey,
Leicester, LE7 7FU, England.
Tel: (00 44) 0116 236 4325
Fax: (00 44) 0116 234 0205**

NEW CASES FOR DOCTOR MORELLE

Ernest Dudley

Young heiress Cynthia Mason lives with her violent stepfather, Samuel Kimber, the controller of her fortune — until she marries. So when she becomes engaged to Peter Lorrimer, she fears Kimber's reaction. Peter, due to call and take her away, talks to Kimber in his study. Meanwhile, Cynthia has tiptoed downstairs and gone — she's vanished without trace. Her friend Miss Frayle, secretary to the criminologist Dr. Morelle, tries to find her — and finds herself a target for murder!

THE EVIL BELOW

Richard A. Lupoff

'Investigator seeks secretary, amanuensis, and general assistant. Applicant must exhibit courage, strength, willingness to take risks and explore the unknown . . . ' In 1905, John O'Leary had newly arrived in San Francisco. Looking for work, he had answered the advert, little understanding what was required for the post — he'd try anything once. In America he found a world of excitement and danger . . . and working for Abraham ben Zaccheus, San Francisco's most famous psychic detective, there was never a dull moment . . .

A STORM IN A TEACUP

Geraldine Ryan

In the first of four stories of mystery and intrigue, *A Storm in a Teacup*, Kerry has taken over the running of her aunt's café. After quitting her lousy job and equally lousy relationship with Craig, it seemed the perfect antidote. But her chef, with problems of his own, disrupts the smooth running of the café. Then, 'food inspectors' arrive, and vanish with the week's takings. But Kerry remembers something important about the voice of one of the bogus inspectors . . .

SPECIAL MESSAGE TO READERS

THE ULVERSCROFT FOUNDATION
(registered UK charity number 264873)

was established in 1972 to provide funds for research, diagnosis and treatment of eye diseases.
Examples of major projects funded by the Ulverscroft Foundation are:-

- The Children's Eye Unit at Moorfields Eye Hospital, London
- The Ulverscroft Children's Eye Unit at Great Ormond Street Hospital for Sick Children
- Funding research into eye diseases and treatment at the Department of Ophthalmology, University of Leicester
- The Ulverscroft Vision Research Group, Institute of Child Health
- Twin operating theatres at the Western Ophthalmic Hospital, London
- The Chair of Ophthalmology at the Royal Australian College of Ophthalmologists

You can help further the work of the Foundation by making a donation or leaving a legacy.
Every contribution is gratefully received. If you would like to help support the Foundation or require further information, please contact:

THE ULVERSCROFT FOUNDATION
The Green, Bradgate Road, Anstey
Leicester LE7 7FU, England
Tel: (0116) 236 4325

website: www.foundation.ulverscroft.com